KU-758-689

**Also By Ann Evans**

Kill Or Die

*For my wife, Heather, thanking her for all her love and support.*
**Robert.**

*And for Wayne, Angie and Debbie with love.*
**Ann**

# Prologue

## Auschwitz 4 August 1944.

'Hexe!' the word rippled around the chamber softly, barely audible, like a breath of wind. They backed off, all of them - the soldiers who had herded these gypsies into the room hours earlier, murmuring the word: Hexe – *Witch!*

Panic glinted in the eyes of the young uniformed men as they shuffled away from her. Witchcraft, there was no other explanation. The woman, perhaps in her forties, maybe younger – they aged quickly here at Auschwitz, those who didn't die – eased herself up from amongst the tangle of naked corpses as if she was rising from the dead. She was naked like the bodies around her, hair shorn to no more than stubble, sallow cheeks and sunken eyes. But very much alive.

The soldiers looked to one another. No one willing to pull their gun and shoot. One soldier ran to fetch the commander. He came in from the August sunshine, peered into the chamber. 'Nicht moglich! Not possible!'

'Hexe!' the word echoed from wall to wall.

Petronella Kytella, mother and widow, had lain down with her young son, cradled him in her arms as the doors clanged shut and gas was pumped in. She'd sang a lullaby softly to him as those around her screamed and tried desperately to claw their way out. She hadn't been afraid to die – saddened, yes, especially for her son, and had marked a circle around them both, a circle and a six-pointed star, as tradition had taught, scratched into the concrete floor with a stone. Then, like her dear son, had closed her eyes and waited for death.

The boy, like everyone else in the room, now lay dead. She would join him very soon. She wondered which of these monsters in their black uniforms would take the pistol from their holster and put a bullet through her head.

The officer who had just entered, snapped out an order. Two younger soldiers stepped over the bodies, grabbed Petronella by her thin arms and dragged her towards the door.

She blinked as the summer sunshine dazzled. They stood her against a wall.

'Warter sie hier!' They marched off.

Head down, Petronella stood with her arms crossed over her nakedness. She wished now that she could pray. To have a God to beg mercy from. But her god was the earth, nature and the seasons. She was a witch, like they'd said, but her work, her beliefs were for the good of others, always. She had never hurt anyone, never wished harm on anyone. Not even these monsters.

The officer returned, carrying a cotton frock and shoes. Not *her* clothing – but clothing. He threw them at her. Confusion washed over her. No bullet?

She dressed quickly, and he grabbed her arm, turning her, marching her towards an armoured car. Hot cracked leather burned her legs but the windows were open as he drove.

Petronella gazed upwards at the blue sky as a warm breeze fanned her face, and wept silently for her son.

### The Fuhrerbunker, Berlin 23 April 1945

Over the winter, news reached Adolf Hitler of a gypsy woman who had survived his gas chamber. It was rumoured she was a white witch. He demanded she be brought to him. His body was growing weaker, another host was needed. This body had served its purpose. The Master would be pleased with the devastation of so many humans.

For so many years now, he had been protected from harm. Harm others would have done to him. But humans were weak, and their ailments crippled their bodies. It was time now to move into another human host and continue the Master's work. And the body of a witch, a white witch, was *perfekt*.

### One week later ...

Petronella Kytella stood before him, unusually tall for a woman, skinny and afraid. But she would become stronger. Once in possession of her body, she would know no bounds. He snapped out a command to the two officers standing guard either side of her, telling them to leave her with him. 'Lass uns in ruhe!'

He circled her, hands behind his back, clasped together to stop the trembling. 'You are a witch?'

'I am of the earth,' she uttered, her eyes downcast.

'You make spells?'

'Yes.'

He stepped closer to her. Looked into her face. Then took her hand in his and brought it up to his lips. 'I have need of you.'

For a second, terror sparked in Petronella Kytella's eyes. She would have run, had there been any place to run to in the small concrete bunker.

Hitler felt himself shudder as the demonic essence, *Lamia*, a spirit that had dwelt in his body all these years, now slipped into Petronella Kytella, filling every crevice of her body like a hand slipping into a silk glove.

The void left inside him was immense. The soul of Adolf Hitler had been crushed by Lamia's dominance many years earlier, like so many before him – Ivan Vasilyevich, Vlad Dracula, Caligula – there had been so many lives, stretching back to day one. But there was still just a shadow of the former Austrian artist and politician still functioning for him to summon the guards.

As clarity returned, he thought back. It was his inauguration as Chancellor in 1933 that had been the moment – he saw that now. He remembered walking amongst the people, shaking so many hands. Which hand had it been?

Now, the pain that Lamia had shielded him from for so many years, protecting him from illness, even assassination attempts, enveloped him. He was vulnerable again. And he knew the world would blame him, Adolph Hitler, for all the atrocities that Lamia had caused through him. The deaths of so many – millions of men, women and children. It was too much to bear, he could not take the agony as he remembered what had been done at his hand – yet through no fault of his own.

But who would believe that? No one.

He forced himself to retain the persona, the one the world knew, to give one last order as the guards returned. 'See she is looked after. Clothed, fed, she is to go to England. See to it!'

*Slipping from the disintegrating body of the man into the woman, Lamia instantly, sensed that this one was different. She felt the resistance of this half-starved female as she inwardly strove to fight off the infiltrator. It was the witch in her, the whiteness, the purity. Well she would not win. The battle for the body and soul of Petronella Kytella had begun, and there would be only one victor – Lamia.*

Petronella felt the attack in every fibre of her being as Hitler touched her. Now looking at him, he visibly shrank, as if racked in pain. Anguish contorted his face, as if his wickedness had caught up with him.

But now she feared for her own soul. There was some parasitic evil crawling through her, trying to control her. Black nothingness swarmed through her head, smothering her consciousness. She fought inwardly to shake free of its hold. Bitterly, she knew she had not the strength to fight it.

As the guards led her away, Petronella glanced back to see Hitler taking a Luger from a desk drawer. Reaching the outer door, the sound of a single gunshot reverberated through the corridors.

The suicide of Adolph Hitler was the last conscious thought of Petronella Kytella. Lamia was reborn.

# Chapter 1

June 1980. Oakwoods, Ashby on the Wold, Surrey.

Something was moving through the long grass. Nine-year-old Paul Christian saw it first, recognised it for what it was. He grabbed his best pal Owen's arm. 'Careful! It's an adder.'

'Where? Oh crikes, you're right.' The bigger, red haired boy grabbed a stick. 'Kill it quick!'

'No way,' Paul said, horrified at the thought. 'They're rare. You never see adders in the wild. Look at it. It's beautiful.'

'It's a bloody snake. Kill it!'

With all his heart Paul wished he'd never mentioned it. Owen wouldn't let it rest. He'd been bored all day, itching to do something. And killing a snake was just his sort of entertainment.

'It's not hurting anyone,' Paul argued.

Owen, a good six months older, taller and heftier than him, sneered. 'You're chicken. Daren't kill a poxy snake.'

'I'm not chicken. I just don't want to hurt it.'

Owen flapped his elbows in and out, making clucking noises. 'Christian is a chicken. Christian is a chicken.'

Paul felt his cheeks starting to burn. 'I'm not!'

'So, prove it.' Owen picked up a rock and pushed it into his hand. 'Go on, smash its head in.'

Paul did his best to stand up to his friend. 'No! That's horrible. And anyway, it's not hurting anyone.'

'So, what's that got to do with anything?' Owen said, hurling another stone at the snake.

Paul grabbed his arm. 'Pack it in, Owen. That's cruel.'

'Pack it in, Owen, that's cruel,' Owen mimicked him. 'What a ponce you are at times.'

1

'I'm not! Anyhow, it's gone now.'

Owen ran a few yards to where the snake had slithered down a hole near an oak tree, then turned back. 'So, if you ain't a chicken, you can prove it another way.' There was mischief written all over his freckled face.

Paul knew what was coming. 'I'm not knocking on her door again. She nearly caught me last time.'

'That's okay,' Owen grinned. 'You can outrun the old hag easily, and while she's off chasing you, I'll sneak in and get a good look at her gold.'

Paul groaned. Owen was convinced the weird old woman who lived in a crabby cottage in the woods had a hoard of Nazi gold stashed away. Once when they'd peeped through her window, they'd spotted something shining like gold on her mantlepiece. Owen had never let it drop.

'I ain't gonna nick it. I just wanna look at it,' said Owen, curling his arm around Paul's shoulder and leading him off towards the cottage.

He didn't like the stranglehold, but at least they were heading away from the snake.

The cottage gave him the creeps. Gravestone grey, with a single small window, like some one-eyed monster watching him. The roof sloped almost to head height, and there was always a crow perched by the chimney. It cawed as they moved stealthily towards the door.

This was their regular pastime, or rather Owen's regular pastime. And if he didn't go along with it, he had to endure Owen's taunts about being too scared, too chicken.

Most times, the old woman ignored them. But once when they'd peered through the window, her face had shot up from inside, ugly and snarling like some demon and they'd nearly crapped themselves.

She'd got a black cat, which seemed appropriate. They joked about her being a witch. There was even a rumour that she'd poisoned a load of local churchgoers just after the war.

She certainly looked like a witch, all in drab, black clothes, and her face was pretty ugly … damn ugly, in fact.

The last time, last Sunday, when they'd been bored, and she'd chased him, Paul had been shocked at how tall she was. Tall and lanky, but boy, could she run. His heart was in his mouth as he'd shot through the trees to escape her. Owen had fled in the opposite direction. They'd met up again later and had a good laugh about it.

'I'm gonna peep through the window,' hissed Owen, as they crept up on the cottage. 'Might see her … you know, doing it with her cat. Her *familiar*. That's what it's called.'

Paul wasn't too sure what he was on about but matched his own leering expression to Owen's as they tip-toed around the side of the building, then ducked down.

'Go on then, knock her door,' Owen hissed, nudging him.

'I will in a minute.'

He jabbed Paul in the ribs. 'Go on, get knocking, and if she chases you, I'm gonna sneak in and look for that gold.'

There was no way out of this without losing face, so taking his courage in both hands, Paul crept up to the front door, rattled the knocker and ran like hell.

She didn't come after him, and eventually he circled back through the woods and met up with Owen again. He hadn't spotted her *doing it* with her cat. He hadn't spotted any gold either. But at least he couldn't call him chicken.

Needing something else to pass the time, Owen decided to build a bonfire.

Paul let him get on with it, and sat on a tree stump in the clearing, whittling a cat from a bit of wood. He wiped the wood sap from the blade of his penknife down his grey shorts. 'You gave me this knife, Owen, for my birthday, remember?'

'Yeah, kind, ain't I?' grinned Owen as he put a match to the kindling. He piled on dry leaves and twigs until it was quite a blaze. 'Hey! Paul, look. It's the old hag's cat.'

A black cat came strolling towards them, tail erect, amber eyes focused on them. There was quite an air about it, like it owned the place. Paul crouched down, calling the cat towards him. 'Here, kitty …'

It ignored him and instead curled itself around Owen's leg. He instantly kicked out. 'Get off me, you mangy creature.' His foot launched the cat into the air.

It landed in the middle of the fire.

Its screeching seemed to bounce from tree to tree, birds took flight. The sound was torturous, like a baby in agony. Frantically, it thrashed about, desperate to escape the flames.

'Get it out! Get it out!' Paul yelled, grabbing a stick and trying to drag the cat out. 'Owen, help me.'

Owen stood back, watching, fascinated. 'Nah, let it burn.'

The screaming stopped, leaving only the crackling of the fire and the smell of burning fur. Paul stared in horror at Owen. 'You've killed it!'

'Good.'

The sound of heavy running footsteps made them spin round. The old woman burst through the woods, a look of hell in her eyes as she took in the scene. And then she screeched. '*Theron!* You killed my cat!'

She picked up a rock.

'Shit! Run!' Owen yelled.

They shot off in opposite directions. Paul ran for his life, but she was right behind him. Glancing back, she was like a mass of swishing blackness, long clothes, long legs, face as ugly as sin, but incredibly nimble for her age.

He didn't see the tree root and in the blink of an eye he was flat on his face in the dirt. He scrambled onto his back just in time to see her towering over him, rock in hand. Frantically, he skittered backwards on his elbows, desperate to get away.

The last thing he saw was her slamming the rock down towards his head.

# Chapter 2

Rear Admiral Paul Christian, formerly of the Royal Navy, and now a leading member of the MOD's Defence Intelligence Agency adjusted the volume of his car radio. *Bad Moon Rising* was playing. He'd always liked the song. He sang along, fingers tapping on the steering wheel as he followed Helena's little yellow Fiat along the winding lanes. They knew the twists and turns well. It was the route they took every weekday morning and evening since leaving the Royal Navy eight years ago. In another mile they parted company. Him north to Westminster and Thames House; his wife north west to Tunbridge.

He saw her head move to the left, glancing back at him through her interior mirror. He blew her a kiss. Another five or six bends and they'd be at the junction and the parting of the ways.

Heading south, the petrol tanker driver reached across to the passenger seat to stroke the fat tortoiseshell cat curled up there. Fat because he spoiled her. She'd turned up at his door six months ago, a scrawny scrap of skin and bone. Perhaps because he'd shown her kindness, she'd become his faithful companion, accompanying him on his trips around the south of England.

With one hand on the wheel and the other stroking the warm ball of fur, he relaxed, knowing the route, enjoying the scenery and the way branches arched overhead forming a sparkling green canopy. He went to draw his left hand back to the steering wheel as he approached the bend.

He hadn't expected pain. He hadn't expected to feel the sudden vicious fangs and claws clamping around his hand. It made him shriek. It made his entire body jerk in shock.

Taking his eyes off the road for a split second he saw the cat was embedded into him, all four feet and mouth clamped around his hand, his blood trickling into her fur. He saw its eyes, intense, determined, hate-filled eyes.

The sway of his tanker made his stomach lurch. With the cat still agonisingly attached to his hand, he tried to grip the wheel, tried to stop the insane swaying of his cargo. Foot on the brake, he heard the screech of his tyres on the road. Saw the little yellow Fiat coming towards him. He was in her path, on her side of the road.

Automatically, he swung the wheel to the left. He saw the Fiat driver's face – she had been smiling to herself. The smile turned into terror as she veered to one side, towards the trees. His cab avoided her but in his wing mirror he saw the angle of the tank, straight across her path.

She hit his trailer at a sideways angle so that her car buckled and crumpled. But for one brief, irrational moment his thoughts weren't on the pretty young driver, dead now probably, mangled in the wreckage of her little yellow car, but on his cat. What the devil had got into her?

The lyrics of the song he'd been enjoyed seemed to scream out their warning about being prepared to die as Paul saw the tanker career around the bend on Helena's side of the road.

The lorry driver was jumping about in his cab like he was having a fit. Paul saw Helena swing her car to the left to avoid the head-on collision. The Fiat reacted well, turning forty-five degrees but the sliding tanker slammed mercilessly into her.

He could hear his own screams as he stamped on his brakes. Helena's car continued its momentum, crumpling, compacting under the massive solid base of the tanker.

Dear God, she couldn't survive this, his wife was petite and gentle and loving. And only an hour ago they had been in bed, had made love, ate breakfast, kissed before getting into their separate cars.

He cried out her name as he stumbled from his car and ran towards the wreckage. In his head he begged God to help, to save her. Let her be okay. The driver was leaping from his cab. Something else shot out, too. Something small and ginger – a cat, maybe. It vanished into the forest.

The smell of burnt rubber and fuel filled the air. Black smoke was billowing from beneath the tanker's base where the crumpled piece of yellow metal had become embedded. And then he saw Helena compacted inside the mess, pressed up against the side window, conscious and screaming.

Reaching her, Paul desperately searched for the door handle, but nothing even resembled a door. Nothing had any shape. Metal was ripped and folded like macabre origami, lodged, immovably under the tanker, crushed against its double back wheels. With all his strength, he pulled at the metal, slicing ribbons of skin and flesh from his hands, while Helena continued to scream, and the black smoke thickened and choked.

First came the sparks, then yellow flames, small at first, flickering out from gaps in the metal, then they burst out, spitting tongues of fire. He heard the whoosh of fuel igniting. He grabbed a rock, smashing it against the side window. It cracked – then someone was pulling him. Big burly arms hauling him backwards, lifting his sixteen-stone clear off the ground and dragging him away from Helena.

He saw her face, heard her shrieks. Felt himself being hurled into the thicket, someone on top of him, the tanker driver he guessed, shielding him from the blast as his world exploded.

# Chapter 3

**July, six years later. Oakwood Residential Home, Ashby on the Wold.**

'Cup of tea, dear?'

The care nurse in her green overall held the beaker in front of the old woman's face. Lifting a thin strand of lank, grey hair, she put the beaker of lukewarm tea to her lips. 'Petronella, dear. Nice cup of tea.'

There was no movement. But then, there never was. In all the years that she'd worked here, she'd rarely seen the old dear do anything but slump in her chair. Yet she managed to keep breathing, somehow. She shifted slightly.

'Ah! That's good, take a sip, my love. How are you this morning?'

There was little response, just a bleak emptiness in her old watery eyes. The nurse held the beaker to Petronella's thin lips and dabbed the dribbles with a tissue.

The eyes of Petronella Kytella looked up into the bloated face hovering over her, while deep inside, the entity that was *Lamia* – a name bestowed upon her by her God, Lucifer – was praying. And her hatred for all that was human, festered.

*Darkness. Life, death. The joy and misery of mankind. The pain they have caused my Master and so the pain he has caused me – the beautiful pain. The torture and the agony. That is the true touch of love. He is the true giver of life, not the creator of souls with a lie of light at their end, and a misplaced love for a creature that only needs to be dominated, ruled and made to do his bidding.*

*How long have I waited, how long have I planned? Yes, since the beginning of life that is as old as my kind has existed. The beginning of man was my beginning. Born to do dark instruction.*

*All the years of human time have I, with my sisters and brothers, walked side by side, silently in the darkness with the cherished on this Earth. They with a blissful ignorance of our existence and true intent as we infiltrate their lives.*

*Our hatred for their souls burns with the fire of hell, and a desire to give them eternal damnation in a putrid pit of never ending pain.*

*Eve gave Adam a new way of life by eating of the forbidden fruit. From bliss to a life of hard labour. The serpent served his Master well that day.*

*Oh, Master of true life, I ask you to open the doors to the demons and dark spells I will need to accomplish a final death blow to the human race.*

*Grant me your anger, so I can reflect it upon this revenge against a God of weakness and naivety that will finally take from Him the cherished souls of His creations and lead them to You, my Master, as bleating sheep.*

*You made me as the start of my kind. And so, I will be the best of my kind, and be the worst that mankind will ever see.*

*And these are the final days ... I have found my means to an end. The time will soon be right, but for now, I play with these souls like a cat plays with a mouse.*

*I ask these things of you, Satan, my Lord.*

# Chapter 4

Paul Christian changed the channel on Sally's car radio. *Bad Moon Rising* was on. He despised the song. He tuned into the classical channel. Chopin was playing. That was more like it.

'Not far now,' Sally Knightly said, casting him an impish smile as she changed down a gear in her vintage E-Type to coast around a bend. 'I'm so nervous, Paul. What if you don't like my home – our home? I'm scared it won't be sophisticated enough for my very own James Bond.'

He smiled. 'James Bond! If only! No, I'm the one who points the James Bonds of this world in the right direction.' He squeezed her thigh. Her skirt was a fine cotton and beneath it, her legs were bare. He had the urge to push the skirt upwards, only that would take her mind off her driving, so he linked his hands in his lap and watched the countryside flying by.

Sally was ten years younger than him and adorable. Straw coloured hair, deep blue eyes that glinted with mischief, and an infectious smile. He was a lucky guy, finding love again after losing Helena. He never thought it possible.

'It's funny, isn't it?' Sally mused, 'you being born so close to where I live now. Quite a coincidence.'

'Coincidence is just a term we use when we can't see the levers and pulleys, or so someone once said,' Paul answered, wanting to tell her to keep her eyes on the road. But it was hardly fair, considering she'd just driven him from London without a hitch. Her driving was fast but faultless. Besides, it wasn't her driving that bugged him, it was other people's. That, and the feeling of not being in control.

Sally cast him a sideways glance. 'So, I wonder who was pulling the strings when we first met all those months ago?'

He smiled at her. 'Who knows? But I have to admit, coming back to live in the place I was born feels a little strange.'

'Fate.' Sally remarked, smiling.

They drove in silence for a while, until village names started to sound vaguely familiar to him. And then landmarks like a church and school and village houses brought back flickerings of recognition.

'This brings back memories. That could have been my old primary school,' he said, trying to picture the house he was born in, but it was nothing but a brick coloured blur.

'You'll have to show me where you were born.'

'I doubt I'd be able to find it now.' He smiled at her. 'Not without a sat nav.'

She laughed. 'Technology! You're out in the wilds, now.'

'I know, and I love it.'

She slowed to take a sharp bend. The road narrowed, trees and hedgerows closing in. 'So, how old were you when your family moved to London?'

'No idea. Pretty young, eight or nine maybe.' But in his head Paul suddenly saw *ten*. Ten in glittery numbers on birthday cards. Ten on silvery deflated balloons.

His thoughts flew back to when he'd woken up in a hospital bed almost forty years ago. There had been a large teddy bear dressed in a number ten football shirt, a pile of unopened presents next to it. *Happy tenth birthday, Paul,* everything cried out as he'd breathed in clinical hospital smells.

His head had felt like a lead weight and there were tubes and wires attached to his body. His parents were sitting beside his bed like waxwork dummies until he spoke. Until he tried to say, 'Is it my birthday already ... how come?' Then their faces had lit up. More than lit up, it was like a box of fireworks had gone off in their motionless grey bodies, exploding them back into life.

'Paul!' They'd cried, repeating his name over and over, tears flooding down their faces. He 'd never seen his dad cry before.

Doctors and nurses had rushed in, flapping around him like he was back from the dead or something.

'Whose birthday is it?' he'd asked, surprised at how hoarse his throat was, as if he hadn't spoken in a long, long time.

'It was yours, my darling,' his mother said, laughing and crying at the same time.

'I'm not ten, mum. I'm not ten till December.' His voice had come out as a croak. He'd felt desperate for a glass of water.

'You *were* ten, Paul,' she said softly. 'You *are* ten.'

'Mum, I'm nine and a half.'

'You're ten, son,' his dad sniffed, taking his hand. 'Ten and a quarter to be precise. You had an accident. You fell and bumped your head. You've been asleep a long time. It's called a coma.'

'How long?' he'd asked, not remembering bumping his head. What did he remember? Not a lot really.

'Almost nine months, son, almost nine months.'

The memory of his father's words echoed through Paul's head as Sally's car turned another sharp bend. It had been years since he'd thought about that day when he had woken up from a coma. He was forty-seven now and the memory came back clear as yesterday.

He put his hand on Sally's thigh again. 'I was ten when we moved away from this area – ten and a quarter to be precise.'

A mile or so further on they veered off the country road onto a narrow lane. A sign indicated 'no through road' and Sally slowed to a crawl. The road was no more than a dirt track and had more twists that the sticks of barley sugar he would buy as a kid – which, weirdly, he could suddenly taste again.

The lane finally opened up alongside a low dry-stone wall smothered in moss and ivy. Sally looked at him, her eyes full of hope. 'Here we are. Home sweet home.'

Paul leaned across and kissed her. 'Well done.'

Her cottage was a mixture of grey stone and red brick, all nooks and crannies with hanging baskets, flowers and lawns, like something from a fairy tale.

The only plant he'd owned was a Peace Lily in a pot and that was plastic. He breathed deeply. 'It's been a long while since I've smelt the countryside, Sal. I'd almost forgotten what it smelled like.'

'You don't suffer from hay fever, do you?'

'We'll soon find out,' he said, spotting a couple of barn-like outbuildings towards the bottom of her garden, beyond which stood a forest. 'You know, I vaguely remember a wood near my old home when I was a kid. I think I may have lived quite close to here.'

'That's Oakwoods.'

The name rang a bell.

'You can cut through the woods to Ashby-on-the-Wold,' she explained. 'I'll show you sometime. But first, I want you to see your new home. Oh, I'm so scared you won't like it.'

He kissed her. 'It's beautiful – as pretty as a chocolate box.'

She took his hand, as happy and eager as a child. He allowed himself to be led up to the front door. As she went to step inside, Paul pulled her back, sweeping her up into his arms. She gasped, then giggled.

'May as well do this right. Okay so we're not exactly married but I want to carry my lover over the threshold. Is that all right with you?'

'Perfect!' She laughed, her arms snaking around his neck.

Paul had to duck to avoid a low beam and as he did, a blinding pain shot through his head from one temple to the other – a burning, searing pain that took his breath away. He staggered, his legs buckling, dropping Sally to her feet as he sank onto his knees.

'Paul!' Sally screamed, as he cradled his head in his hands, the pain shooting through him like stabbing needles.

Eyes squeezed shut, he saw nothing except a blinding red haze. As if coming from far away he heard Sally's frantic cries, sobbing now.

Gradually, the excruciating pain eased. As if the needles were being withdrawn. As suddenly as the pain had hit him, it had gone. Sally clung to him, trembling. 'It's okay, I'm okay.'

'Did I do that?'

'No, of course you didn't. I must have trapped a nerve as I ducked my head. It was just a sharp pain, it took me by surprise. I'm sorry I scared you.'

She looked with big soulful puppy-dog eyes. 'Are you sure? Should I get a doctor?'

'No honestly, no need. I'm absolutely fine.'

She looked doubtful and held onto him as if he might shatter like some delicate bone china figurine.

'Really Sal, I'm good to go. Ready for the conducted tour.' It was probably ungrateful to shrug her hands off him, but he felt stupid collapsing like that, and puzzled. Annual medical checks had shown no lasting effects from the coma all those years ago. Maybe it had been just a trapped nerve.

She led the way through to the kitchen. The floor was old-fashioned red tiles, the sort of floor you'd pay a fortune for these days; sturdy oak furniture, garden flowers in vases.

Her face screwed up in anticipation. 'You hate it, don't you?'

He pulled her close, breathing in her scent. 'I love it. It's perfect.'

'You're not just saying that?'

His answer was to kiss her, and she wrapped her arms around his neck, returning his kiss with the promise of much more. 'Where's the bedroom?' he murmured against her lips.

'We haven't got your cases in yet.'

'They can wait. I can't.'

Her eyes, slightly mascara-smudged from tears, glinted with seduction. She took his hand and led the way up the ridiculously narrow staircase, her perfectly rounded buttocks swaying before his eyes, mesmerizing. Bare calves, ever so slightly tanned, neat little slip-on flat shoes in sky blue.

The bedroom was as pretty as the rest of the house. It smelled of her and the double bed was so soft, it swallowed them up.

There was little foreplay, his need wouldn't wait. Nothing, in fact, would wait.

They lay in each other's arms, with him guessing that was probably the world record in the art of speed love-making. 'Sorry. Bit too excited.'

Her fingers stroked his chest. 'I'm not complaining.'

He stared up at the ceiling – noticing a spider. 'We've got company.'

She followed his gaze, but rather than screaming like Helena would have, she shrugged. 'I'll put it outside in a minute.'

'*You* will?'

'They don't bother me.'

'Good! You've got the job.'

She turned wide-eyed. 'Don't tell me you're scared of spiders.'

'Not scared. Just not too keen.'

'Ha! Is Paul Christian, M15's second in command at the DIA, scared of spiders? I don't believe it!'

His eyebrows arched. 'Have you seen the size of it?'

'Wuss,' she laughed, wriggling onto her knees to plant a kiss on his nose before rolling off the bed. 'Come on, I need a cup of tea. Where did you throw my knickers?'

He wasn't surprised to find that Sally made tea using a teapot when he finally got downstairs. The way her cheeks blushed when he teased her about it, delighted him.

'So, what's in the barns? I'm half imagining you keep chickens and ducks and things.'

'I wish. I do have Bluebell though – wherever she is.'

'And Bluebell is …?'

'My cat. She turned up about four years ago. Lord knows where she came from. I had a cat flap made, she just comes and goes as she pleases. She's so intelligent, almost like she knows what you're thinking.'

Shit. Hate cats, Paul thought, keeping his smile firmly in place. There was something about them that freaked him out. He glanced at the cat flap wondering if he could jam the hinge shut.

Guilt swamped him. This beautiful, sexy, loving young woman was sharing her home with him. More than that, giving him a new life, one he never thought he'd get. The least he could do was get on with her cat. Cute name, Bluebell. Just a pity it wasn't a dog.

Want to see our workroom?' Sally asked. 'I've made some space and bought some new office furniture. Come and see.'

It was a hexagonal-shaped conservatory overlooking the back garden. The room smelled of leather. He whistled. 'This place is a Tardis!'

'Isn't it just! This is where I do my designs.' There was a drawing board, two large tables, one with an industrial sewing machine clamped to it; rolls of leather in various colours, shelves full of packaging and a rail of designer style leather bags. 'And over this side …' She made a sweeping gesture. '… Is your desk, filing cabinets and swivelly chair. Is it okay?'

'I hadn't expected this. I just thought me and my laptop would perch somewhere.'

'As if. You'll have to set up your own internet server and stuff. And no doubt some special Skype links or whatever you people do.'

'You, Sally Knightly, are an amazing young woman. But you can leave all that side of things to me. And I'm sorry I can't talk more about my work …'

'I know! I know! Official Secrets and all that. Don't worry. I'm fine with it all.'

'Good,' he said, planting a kiss on the top of her head. He wandered over to her working area. 'So, these are your designer bags? Nice.'

'And made with only the finest Italian leather, I'll have you know.'

'I'll buy one from you for my mother's birthday. She's knocking on a bit but still a slave to fashion.'

Sally looked curiously at him. 'She's still alive? You've never spoken about your parents. I assumed they were dead.'

'Dad is. Lung cancer did him in years ago.'

'Will you take me to meet your mother, sometime?'

'Absolutely. Next time I visit her.' To his surprise, Sally turned away to stare out the window. He was astute enough to recognise when a woman was feeling hurt about something. He stood behind her and wrapped his arms around her waist. 'She'll love you.' She made no response. 'Sal, what are you thinking?'

She shrugged. 'It's stupid. Here we are moving in together and I know nothing about the important things in your life – your parents, your childhood. You don't talk about them. I can understand you not wanting to talk about Helena, but I'd love to hear what you were like as a boy.' She turned in his arms to face him. 'Were you a podgy little thing always grazing your knees, or a brainbox, with your head stuck in a book? I bet you were, that's why you've got such a good job now.'

'A bit of both probably. I liked school. I was fortunate to have a public school education, then University and the Royal Naval College; eleven years in Naval Intelligence – but you know all this, Sal.'

'I mean when you were little?' she pressed. 'When you were a little boy.'

He gazed over the top of her head, to the garden and the barns. 'Well, I reckon I must have been a clumsy little kid at times. But I can't remember, Sal. It was such a long time ago, and does it matter? It's the future that counts now.'

She sighed. 'You're right, I suppose. And it'll be fun discovering each other bit by bit, revealing the layers, stripping away the secrets.' Blue eyes sparkling with mischief, she began unbuttoning his shirt.

His hand clasped over hers and he nodded towards the outbuildings at the bottom of the garden. 'What's out there?'

'Come and see!'

He followed her into the garden, smiling to himself at the way she had a skip to her walk. She really was a breath of fresh air after the harsh cynical world of politicians, diplomats and red tape.

There was a patio and a twisted old yew tree that reached up to the bedroom window. Wild bird feeders hung from tree branches, butterflies and birds seemed to be everywhere.

He laughed. 'Snow White springs to mind!'

She pulled a face. 'It's twee, isn't it? Very girly. I bet you hate it.'

'I love it. It's so *you*. It's pretty and generous and, and I'm overwhelmed.'

Casting him a half disbelieving glance she linked his arm and led him towards the outbuildings.

There were two barns. One held all her gardening tools – lawn mower, rakes, spades, watering cans; the other, however, was something else.

The barn door was on a latch and creaked on rusted hinges as Sally opened it. He'd expected it to be dark and dingy and full of junk, but sunlight streaked through the windows despite them being caked in grime and cobwebs. There was a workbench and a wood turner's lathe beneath a tarpaulin. Nearby was a stone-grinder to sharpen tools and a generator to power everything. Attached to the walls was an array of carpentry tools. He lifted one of the chisels from its rack and felt the steely sharpness against his thumb.

'Unbelievable.' he said, breathing in the faint lingering smells of cut wood. 'Don't tell me you're a carpenter as well.'

'No. This was all here when I bought the cottage about nine years ago.' Standing in the centre of the high-ceilinged barn, with the sunlight on her, she looked like she was on a stage, the spotlight highlighting her beauty. 'This house had been vacant for a while when I bought it. I guess the previous owner was a craftsman. I imagine if the windows were scrubbed this would make a great workshop.'

Paul strolled around the barn, impressed by its spaciousness and the warmth of the sunlight and the glorious smells of timber.

He picked a piece of wood from the floor, just a piece the size of his hand and felt the rough texture of bark against his skin. His thoughts flew backwards.

He was staring down at small grubby hands whittling away at a piece of wood with a penknife. The knife had three blades and a corkscrew, and the middle of the handle was inlaid with red plastic. He was sitting on the stump of a tree in short trousers, pumps and grey socks. And Owen was building a bonfire.

# Chapter 5

That evening Sally cooked dinner. A real home-cooked meal using vegetables that she'd grown in her garden and beef from the local butcher – she'd delighted in telling him. He devoured every mouthful like it was nectar. Life once again held hope. Incredible when, at one time, all hope had gone.

Now he held a brandy glass in his hands and breathed in its rich aroma as the logs crackled in the fireplace and orange flames danced and flickered before his eyes.

Sally eased herself from the sofa and kissed the top of his head. 'I'm going to wash the dishes.'

'No, I'll do it later,' he protested but she just smiled.

'Relax. I hope you're not too warm, I just love a crackling fire, even in summer.'

He gazed after her. 'I'm in heaven!'

The sounds of Sally busying herself around her kitchen was music to his ears. For too long he'd endured television programmes he didn't really want to watch, volume turned up to banish the silence. Or worse, to mask the sound of screaming. He heard Helena's screams less and less now. Since meeting Sally, hardly at all.

He sipped the brandy, it warmed his throat and made him drowsy. He drifted, eyes half closed, listening to the crackling of burning logs. Tomorrow he would get a bucket of soapy water and wash down the windows in the barn, inside and out. Maybe get a broom and give the place a good old spring clean. His mind wandered to that penknife, recalling now that he'd got it for his ninth birthday. It had been a gift from Owen.

The charred logs shifted in the grate and Paul half opened his eyes. He stared into the fire. Vivid red and blue tongues of flame licked upwards, the heart of the fire glowed now like some magical palace. He could see gateways and portcullises. He could see images in the flames.

He awoke suddenly and tried not to look. He wanted to tear his gaze away, but it was too late. His brain conjured up a face amongst the burning embers. A shrieking face, wide-eyed with terror. A face lying sideways at a painfully twisted angle as Helena burned to death. And the screaming was back.

In bed later that night, Paul made love to Sally again. This time it was gentle and slow, leading gradually into a passion that consumed them both. As they fell back against the pillows, the sighs that escaped their lips were ones of satisfaction.

The bed was far more comfortable than the one he had in London, and all the sounds of the countryside were keeping sleep at bay. Laying back on his pillow with Sally's arm across his chest he could see a crescent moon through the window. Gazing at it, he tried to distinguish the different noises of the night. Squeaks coming from outside could be rodents, mice or voles maybe, and the louder high-pitched cries made him think that some poor rabbit had fallen prey to a fox.

'Are you listening to it all?' he murmured. 'I heard an owl – an owl, Sally! Can you believe that?'

'I've seen him,' Sally murmured, not opening her eyes. 'He's a beautiful barn owl. And those gruff grunting sounds, that's a badger.'

'You'd think the night would be silent, but it's as noisy as hell.'

She chuckled. 'Wait till you hear the dawn chorus!'

The bedroom window was open, and the breeze gently rustled the open curtains. It was then that Paul heard the scraping, tapping sound against the window pane for the first time.

As if sensing the sudden tensing of his muscles, Sally's fingers stroked his chest. 'And that's just the tree, talking to me.'

Paul looked at her.

She opened one eye and smiled. 'I'm not joking. The yew tree likes to whisper its secrets to me.'

'How much wine did you have?'

Sally mischievously tweaked his nipple. 'I'm not drunk or mad. Listen.'

'I'm listening.' But all he could hear were the uneven tapping sounds of wood against glass.

'There!' said Sally. 'Hear that? Pa…ul…Christ..ian. It knows your name.'

He did his best to tune into whatever woodland FM world she was listening to, but heard only the scratch, scratch, scratch sound as the breeze blew twigs and leaves across the glass. In the end he burst out laughing. 'You're the Doctor Dolittle of the tree world. What's that song, 'I talk to the trees, but they don't listen to me. I know a man in a white coat who might though.'

Sally dived on top of him, jabbing him with soft prods and pinches until he was curled up into a ball, laughing and doing his best to fend her off. He won after rolling on top of her and holding her wrists above her head in one hand.

'Okay, Tree Girl, now what are you going to do?'

'Mock, if you like,' she said, lying passively beneath him. 'But it's true. The tree even told me that we were meant to be.'

He rolled off her. 'Go on, I'm intrigued.'

She sat up, the moonlight making her naked skin glow, highlighting the silhouette of her breasts. Paul lay propped up on one elbow, indulging her little fantasy. In fact, the way she looked at that moment, he would have indulged her anything.

There was excitement in her voice, as if this was something she'd been dying to tell him but had never found the right moment, until now.

'After I'd first met you, and I'd come back here from London wondering if you would call me, like you'd promised, I heard the tree whispering to me. *He's the one.* That's what the scratching said, honestly Paul, it said: *He's the one, he's the one, he's the one …* '

# Chapter 6

Paul couldn't wait to make a start on the barn after he'd woken up. Firstly though, he contacted his office at Thames House to organise for the IT techs to work their magic. Once communications were working as they should, he dealt with the most urgent messages, not letting it bug him that he was supposed to be having a few days off to get his new home sorted. Besides, it was a delight to have Sally beavering away in the same room. She had a knack of knowing when he was concentrating on work and wasn't to be disturbed. But occasionally she would stand behind him and massage his neck as he deftly rattled out messages and made calls. For her own part, she was working on some new designs. She was producing ten new shoulder bags in seven colours, she'd explained to him after breakfast.

She was still hard at it as Paul pressed 'send' to his last email and closed down his computer. Leaving Sally with a cup of tea, he changed into his oldest pair of jeans and the least expensive pair of shoes he owned, rolled up his shirt sleeves and headed eagerly towards the barn.

As he opened the barn door, it seemed to emit a long drawn out sigh. As if it had been waiting with baited breath. He smiled at the fanciful notion. It couldn't have known he intended sprucing it up – unless, of course, the yew tree had told it.

He stepped inside, breathing in its smells, seeing the dust particles floating in the light rays through murky windows. It was a long, high barn with four windows at either side, and on the end wall, to his surprise, because he hadn't spotted it yesterday, hung an axe.

Like a focal feature it seemed to take pride of place. He walked slowly towards it. It was, in true woodcutter style, a genuine forestry axe. The handle was a four feet long piece of shaped ash, its grain sanded and polished to a deep gloss. The blade was gleaming honed steel, its cutting edge as sharp as a razor. It was hard to imagine it had been hanging here, gathering dust for nine years. He ran his hand along the handle. There was no dust.

Cautiously, and aware that his heart was thudding, Paul lifted the axe down from its brackets. It was weighty but not too heavy and his hands fitted snugly into the curves and indentations of the wood. It could almost, he thought irrationally, have been hand-made for him.

He carried the weighty object out of the barn, liking the sensation of handling this primaeval-like tool. He had a few practice swings, it had been a while since he'd handled a weapon like this. It wasn't something to mess about with. This axe needed treating with respect.

Readjusting his stance and double-checking that neither Sally nor anyone else was around to get decapitated by his novice actions, he raised the axe to shoulder height and brought it thudding down into the earth. It left a gaping hollow as he pulled it free. Leaning it against the barn wall, he found a small log and placed it carefully on a stump that was clearly meant for the job. It sliced perfectly in two.

The prospect of cleaning windows lost some of its appeal after using the axe, but Paul stuck to his good intentions, and eventually placed it back on its brackets and fetched a bucket of soapy water and a sponge from the house.

An hour's work brought the windows up sparkling clean. Then a good brushing from one end of the barn to the other turned the whole place into a workshop that had distinct possibilities.

He couldn't quite put his finger on when the notion first occurred to him. It might have been when he'd just finished washing the windows and the room was bathed in dazzling sunlight – or maybe it was when he was brushing the old sawdust away. But most probably it had been when he first picked up the axe.

It was, he had to admit, a pie in the sky notion. Yet the prospect filled him with unbelievable excitement. He hadn't the skill nor the knowhow. He'd be stupid to think otherwise. The only thing he'd ever whittled were stick figures. He remembered now the object he'd been whittling with his penknife as a kid. It had been an animal, a dog or cat. It was hard to tell – although he had the vague feeling that it had been a cat. But basically, it was little more than a stick with four stumpy legs, a head and a tail.

Anyway, there was no harm in getting the whole place in good working order, and so he set about the generator next, discovering with glee there was petrol in a can, and that it still worked, as did the grinder and the lathe. There was even a small kiln at the rear of the barn. The mechanical whirr of machinery brought Sally to the conservatory window. She leant out. He heard her voice as he finally turned the machinery off.

'Does it all still work?' she shouted.

'Seems to. Don't laugh, but I'm going to try my hand at this carpentry malarkey. Reckon it will be okay to get a few chunks of wood from the forest – fallen stuff? I'm not planning on chopping down any mighty oaks and have the forestry commission on my back.'

'There's plenty of it. Have fun!'

He went back into the barn, walking purposely towards the axe on the far wall. Reverently, he lifted it down and, resting it over his shoulder, he turned and strode out into the sunshine, feeling like some Nordic warrior of yesteryear.

It was cooler amongst the trees. The massive ash, birch and oak trees spread their branches to form leafy green parasols that shielded earth dwellers from the burning midday sun, he thought whimsically. The glimpse of a grey squirrel scampering across his path delighted him, although he had to admit, you could see squirrels just as easily in Hyde Park.

Walking further, loving the freedom, loving the solitude, he breathed deeply, filling his lungs with the smell of ferns and wild garlic instead of exhaust fumes and takeaways. Beneath his feet were seasons of dead leaves, cushioning his steps, and occasionally there came a started clap of wings as a wood pigeon lost its nerve and flew to higher branches as he invaded its space.

He'd walked far enough and the urge to put the axe to good use was rising. He looked around for logs or fallen branches. Ignoring the wood that had fungi living in its cracks, or smothered in moss or held fast by brambles, he walked on.

The sight of what seemed to be a massive disc-like structure with tentacles bigger than him sprouting from its circumference, literally stopped him in his tracks.

He saw at once what it was, an uprooted tree – an uprooted oak. A massive uprooted oak that seemed to have just keeled over and died. Although some roots were still attached, and fresh growth evident on lower branches. The weight of this sixty-foot-tall monster had levered up most of its roots as it had crashed down, and a small crater lay at its base, layered with last autumn's leaves.

It had brought down other trees, forming what looked to Paul like a tragic woodland graveyard. For long moments he stood, leaning on his axe thinking what a terrible shame it was that this magnificent oak had fallen like this.

Maybe there'd been a storm, or it was diseased, and the roots had weakened. He didn't know, he was no expert in arboretum matters – or anything to do with nature really. When he was a kid maybe …

He'd loved the forest, hadn't he? Messing about, climbing trees – him and Owen. Yes, he was positive he'd done that. Maybe this oak was one he'd climbed at some time in the past. At some point before he was nine and a half and his world turned black.

He didn't remember bumping his head so badly it put him in a coma for nine months. What he did remember was whittling a cat from a little piece of wood with the penknife that his best friend Owen had given him. He remembered sitting on a tree stump, concentrating on not pressing too hard on the blade in case he chopped the cat's tail or leg off. And he remembered Owen building a bonfire.

Paul picked his way amongst the massive branches, choosing a section where the wood was only the thickness of Sally's waist. He gauged what he wanted to chop off. Big enough to try and carve something from, but not too big that he couldn't carry it home.

He raised his axe, stupidly apologising to the tree for taking such liberties, and brought it down. It cut deftly into the bark and refused to come out. There was definitely a skill to this that he certainly hadn't mastered. But practice makes perfect, so they say, and determinedly he wangled the blade out, raised the axe again, took aim and made another decisively clean slice into the branch.

He was sweating by the time he'd cut off the chunk he wanted. Damp patches discoloured his shirt and even his jeans were sticking to him. Looking at the severed piece of wood, he hoped he hadn't been too ambitious. But he felt elated. This was as good as a session in the gym – and a lot more fun.

# Chapter 7

S ally was watching for him. Emerging from the woods, axe over one shoulder, chunk of wood under his arm, he spotted her at the kitchen doorway. She waved and went back indoors.

Leaving the log and the axe by the barn wall, he was desperate for a drink, a gallon of cold water ought to do the trick.

'I was just about to send out a search party!' Sally said, removing tinfoil from two plates of cheese, pickle and crusty bread.

He gulped down two glasses of water. 'Have you missed me?'

'Of course,' she said carrying the plates out to the patio table. 'Bring some beers, will you?'

He downed another glass of water and grabbed two beers from the fridge.

'I was beginning to think you'd got lost in the woods. I was half expecting a phone call saying you'd ended up in the village and would I come and pick you up.'

'I haven't been gone that long, have I? Must admit I haven't looked at my watch once.' He did so now, surprised that it was mid-afternoon.

'You've been gone three hours.' Her smile was slightly strained. 'What on earth have you been doing?'

He pressed a finger to his temple, to the spot where the needles had jabbed him yesterday. 'Exploring, chopping wood. Time flies when you've enjoying yourself.'

'Okay, and what do you intend doing with that great big chunk of wood you've brought back?'

He found the cheese and pickle delicious and would rather have concentrated on eating than talking. Still, she deserved some kind of explanation – except he didn't have one.

'That's my practice piece,' he said, brushing crumbs off his shirt, surprised as a sparrow hopped right up to his feet to feast on them. 'I'm just going to mess around with it, get some practice with the lathe. See what emerges. A pile of sawdust I imagine.'

She laughed. 'You might surprise yourself.'

'Maybe I will.'

After their late lunch Paul checked his emails, slightly irritated that various matters needed attending to before he could get back to the barn. He forced himself to concentrate on work. It was beginning to look as if the World Peace Conference planned for November was actually going to happen. He could hardly believe that the Government had come up with a strategy that might get the President of the USA and world leaders from the Middle East, North Africa and a host of other countries as well as those known terrorist factions, all sitting down around the table and talking to each other. In a way he could hardly dare believe it would work. Hadn't there only ever been one time during the history of mankind when there had been no wars on earth – at the birth of Christ?

So, unless there was to be a second coming, he doubted it would succeed. Not that he voiced his doubts. He would remain positive. After all, miracles did happen occasionally. He only had to look at his new relationship with Sally to realise that. The fact that he'd found love and happiness again – now that was a *real* miracle.

After dealing with his correspondence and more phone calls, he finally allowed his thoughts to return to matters of a more relaxing nature. Armed with a litre bottle of water, he strolled back to the barn.

The piece of wood was around twenty-four inches in diameter and about seven inches deep. It was light oak with a thick, rough, dark bark. He lifted it close to his face, liking the smell and the silkiness of its inner texture. Taking it inside, he placed it on a revolving disc bolted to the workbench. He examined it from all angles, seeing if it cried out to be turned into some glorious piece of art. He finally had to admit to himself that it looked like a chopped bit of wood from a fallen tree.

He had no idea whether you could carve freshly cut wood. It probably needed to be dried. Maybe that was what the kiln was for. But his lack of understanding was overridden by his exuberance to have a go.

He took a chisel from the rack. The handle was worn smooth by some artisan of bygone days, yet his own hands seemed to slip into the contours. With a tingle of excitement, he touched the blade against the wood.

He had no training in carpentry – couldn't even remember doing it at school – but glided the metal lightly over the centre of the log, hoping he was doing it right. A slither of wood shaving curled up and along the blade. He repeated the action, ending the cut – like before – at the central point. He made another cut and then another, moving the log anti-clockwise as he worked until he had formed a full circle of grooves. He blew away the curls and examined his efforts. It wasn't much to look at, but he was enjoying the work. There was something therapeutic about it. Almost like he was running on autopilot, almost like he was a natural.

By the time Sally wandered down to tell him dinner was ready, he must have looked like a demon barber standing knee deep in shorn locks. As for his chunk of wood, it was now vaguely resembling some sort of fruit bowl.

'Hello,' she said slowly, wrapping her arms around his waist and looking at his creation. 'Wow! That's not bad for a first attempt. It's a bowl, right?'

'It certainly is. The splinters are extra.'

Paul reached for a smaller chisel, hoping to smooth away some of the roughness, but Sally's hand came and rested over his. 'Won't you leave off now and come in for dinner? I've hardly seen you all day.'

For a second he felt a twinge of annoyance. He didn't want to stop. He honestly felt like he could whittle away all night – although he'd need a powerful halogen lamp, one that gave a good spread of light. He'd think about that tomorrow.

'I've made chicken breasts stuffed with Gruyere cheese and wrapped in Parma ham, and the wine is chilling.'

'Have I time for a shower?'

'You certainly have.' She wrinkled her nose, making no bones about the fact that he stank. 'A priority, I'd say.'

He slapped her bottom. 'Cheeky minx.'

Laughing, she put some of the tools he'd been using back in the rack then took his hand, leading him out of the barn. He was amazed to see the sun so low in the sky. He hadn't noticed. As he closed the barn door an odd feeling of regret washed over him. A feeling of loss, as if he was leaving someone or something behind.

'Should I light the fire tonight? Or is it too warm?'

'No, don't bother with it tonight, Sal.' He didn't relish a repeat of last night's illusions. 'Keep it for autumn evenings. I'll soon warm you up if you feel chilly.'

She glanced up almost demurely. 'I like the sound of that.'

# Chapter 8

Five days after Paul's arrival Bluebell finally made an appearance. Sally had started to worry about her cat not returning for its meals, while he was secretly hoping it had found a new home.

But then it appeared.

He was in bed, lying on his back, fast asleep. A weight on his chest had stirred him. His dream told him it was Sally, her fingers walking up his torso from stomach to chest. But as he slowly came awake and sensed she was fast asleep on her side with her back to him, his eyes shot open.

It stood on his chest. A pair of luminous cat eyes staring straight into his. Only the moonlight through the window outlining its feline shape stopped him from reacting, stopped him from flinging the damn thing to the floor.

*It was just a cat.* Not a demon, just a cat – Bluebell. But he was cautious. Cold sweat suddenly oozed from every pore in his body. A trickle ran past the corner of his eye and tickled his ear. He could see his startled face reflected in the cat's eyes and something at the back of his mind stirred. Instantly he was swamped with feelings of remorse, guilt … *horror.*

The cat hissed, eyes narrowing, teeth bared as if it was facing some predator. Then it sprang down from his chest. Paul jerked from the force of its hind legs pushing against his ribcage as it leapt off him and shot out of the room.

He sat bolt upright, heart thudding. The feelings of revulsion and sadness were still in his head, in his heart. But whatever had instigated them was buried deeply in his subconscious.

He struggled to bring the memory to the forefront of his mind, but it was embedded far too deeply to be recalled.

Paul's first few weeks in his new home flew by. Considering the cat's initial fear of him, Bluebell didn't stay away for too long. She turned up regularly for meals and often curled up on Sally's lap, even when she was machining leather. Not once did she try and sit on his lap however, for which he was grateful.

His week was split, Tuesdays to Thursdays in London, Friday and Monday working from home, and weekends blissfully were his. But of course, a phone call from head office could change all that in an instant and frequently did.

He travelled by train unless they sent a car to pick him up. The station was just on the outskirts of the village, so Sally usually drove him there and he would walk back on his return.

Travelling home one Thursday evening in August, he realised the tingle of excitement he felt wasn't just the prospect of being with Sally again, but of getting on with his woodcarving.

He actually *loved* the hours he spent roaming the forest for suitable chunks of wood for whittling and carving. The therapeutic feel of a rough piece of timber gradually becoming satin smooth filled him with inexplicable joy. He had no idea where this passion had come from, but he was glad of it. And he was getting pretty damn good at it, even if he said so himself.

The first attempts at a fruit bowl, which had become a potpourri holder because of the splinters, had long since been improved upon. A second bowl – which *was* used for fruit – now sat on the sideboard, full of fresh fruit from the garden. There was also a plant pot holder, a walking stick because the slender piece of wood had demanded it, and his latest, almost finished project, a cross.

The cross was an off-cut from a disastrous attempt at a trellis-shaped key holder. The off-cut had lain discarded amongst the sawdust and wood shavings. He hadn't noticed it until sweeping up at the end of the day.

It was just a couple of inches long, slightly less wide, with the most perfect wood grain pattern running through it.

It had been effortless to carve. It was simply a matter of gently sanding away the husk to reveal the beauty within. It came as an afterthought to drill a hole at the top, so a chain or tie could be threaded through and it could be worn around the neck.

The cross so far, was his most prized and beautiful piece of woodwork.

Four weeks after first moving in with Sally, the parish priest – Father Willoughby – came by for a visit. Sally was an avid church-goer, and while she'd dragged him along to the church of St Mary Magdalene once, he'd wormed his way out of attending any services since. Not that it wasn't a beautiful church, with the Passion of Christ depicted in its stained-glass windows, it was just that, since Helena died, it was hard to give praise to a God who had ignored his desperate prayers that day.

Father Wallace Willoughby was a diminutive man and the sight of him standing in the open barn doorway with the sun at his back made Paul think, for one irrational moment, that he was being visited by an elf.

It was the familiar – once heard never forgotten, boom of a voice from such a little fellow that assured Paul that he wasn't seeing things.

'As was the Son of God a carpenter, so you follow in his footsteps.'

'Father Willoughby, good to see you,' Paul said, blowing away a layer of fine dust from his latest creation.

There was a glint of sunlight on the priest's round, Lennon-like glasses. 'I trust I'm not disturbing you. I was just passing.'

Paul smiled to himself. No one *just passed* this place.

The priest's gaze fell on the cross that lay with other pieces Paul had crafted. His eyes widened. 'Now this is one fine work of art.'

'It's not bad, is it? Here, feel; smooth as the proverbial baby's ...'

Father Willoughby's stubby hand enveloped the cross, feeling its weight, its texture. Then gazing at it, murmured. 'Beautiful! Primitively beautiful!'

'Primitively?' Paul mused, caught off guard by the priest's reaction.

'Why, yes. Breathe that earthy smell, caress the feel of the wood. It is from the earth but reformed by the hand of man, now an adornment to praise God. It is beautiful. Primitive and beautiful.'

'It's yours,' Paul said, startling himself. He would never have dreamed of giving away his fruit bowls. No one in their right mind would want one of them. But this – this was something to cherish. He'd sensed that himself, and the little priest had confirmed it.

'I'm touched. Can I pay you for it?' His hand was already in his pocket.

'Absolutely not!' Paul stopped him. 'It's my pleasure.' And it was. Never had he felt such a rush of joy at giving something that he had made to another human being. It was a weird sensation.

Sally joined them, taking in the situation, her mouth fell open. 'You made this?'

'Yup!' He smiled. 'I can't believe I'm enjoying this so much. Don't know why I didn't take it up years ago.'

'It's lovely!' said Sally.

'Primitively beautiful, according to the good Father here.'

Her eyes sparkled. 'A bit like you, darling ...'

He laughed. 'Absolutely!'

Father Willoughby cleared his throat. 'I'll find myself a chain to thread through, and wear it under the old dog collar. There's terrible wickedness in this world – terrible.' He stepped closer to them both, one hand clutching the cross, his other hand pointing to Paul's heart. 'Protecting oneself from evil is what we all ought to be doing. And a hand-made wooden cross seems a grand way of keeping one's spiritual armour up to par. I suggest you make one for your good lady, and one for yourself.'

Paul gave a vague nod of agreement, hoping they weren't in for another of his hell fire and brimstone sermons – which had been another reason he hadn't gone back to church with Sally.

Reading his mind, Sally changed the subject. 'Can I get anyone a drink? Tea, coffee, beer?'

They had coffee on the patio, Paul had a beer, and Father Willoughby did his level best not to turn a chat into an interrogation. Paul recognised the visit for what it was, and went with the flow. It wasn't a bad thing to find out who was living in your neighbourhood. In a way he quite admired the little priest for asking so many questions.

Turning the inquisition around, when Paul felt he'd given away enough about himself, he learned that Father Willoughby had been at St Mary Magdalene's for fourteen years.

'Our church is steeped in history,' Father Willoughby went on, helping himself to another chocolate biscuit and dipping it into his coffee. 'Sadly, some of it tragic.'

'That's the church for you,' Paul remarked.

'Careful now, Paul,' warned the priest. 'Don't blacken its character as a whole just because of one tragedy.'

Paul took another mouthful of cold beer before asking what he meant. Not that he was particularly interested, but it was so obviously a leading statement.

'You don't know?' said Father Willoughby. 'You haven't heard of the Pentecost Sunday tragedy of 1947?'

Sally leaned forward. 'When everyone in church died? That's just a myth, isn't it?'

Paul raised one eyebrow, marginally curious, but more eager to get back to his woodwork. From here he could see right into the barn to where sunlight was glinting off the axe head, beckoning him, pulling him back, reminding him he had work to do.

Sally touched his hand. 'Did you ever hear that story, Paul … when you were a little boy?'

'Don't think so.' He finished his beer, wanting to push his chair back, say thank you, it's been great, and get back to his wood carvings. He stayed put.

'Oh, it's a horrendous story if it was true,' Sally continued, perched on the edge of her chair. 'I did some research on the area when I first moved here. The Communion hosts had been poisoned. People died in agony.'

Paul frowned as something jabbed in his brain, disturbing some long, lost memory. Yes, he did vaguely recollect something about a massacre in their local church. It was a tale he'd heard long ago, before he was nine and a half and his world turned black.

'As I just said, evil is never far away,' said the priest. 'You must be on your guard. That one incident, terrible though it was, had far reaching consequences. It made everyone for miles around too afraid to take Holy Communion. It's taken generations to rebuild confidence in the Sacraments. The devil was certainly doing a jig for joy in those days.'

'Did they find out who did it?' Sally asked, frowning.

'Some say it was the priest himself. That he'd gone insane.' Father Willoughby dunked another biscuit in his coffee and left it to dissolve into a floating scum. 'Personally, I believe it was the work of Lucifer himself.'

Paul raised his eyebrows. He'd heard enough of this religious mumbo jumbo. 'It's more likely to be the work of man than mystic.'

'Man, yes!' said the priest. 'Absolutely a man – or a woman – who administered that poison, but under whose influence? Who was the controlling force behind those actions?' His voice rose to its usual bellow. 'Ask yourselves that question. Who – or *what* – was the controlling force?'

Paul didn't know the answer, besides he'd got better things to think about. But the priest was getting into a stride. Paul heaved a sigh, guessing he was in for an afternoon of preaching. There was no avoiding it. He hadn't gone to church, so the church had come to him.

# Chapter 9

## August 2018, Oakwood Residential Home

Her breathing was shallow, her skin wrinkled, sagging, cold and clammy to the touch. The nurse brushed a strand of long grey hair from Petronella's sleeping face. She doubted the old lady would still be alive by morning – although she'd thought that practically every night since she started working here. Petronella was a tough old bird, that was for sure. Not one to give in. 'Good night, dear,' the nurse whispered, turning off the light, and closing the bedroom door.

Not asleep – never asleep. Vacating for a while that old decaying body. Leaving it sleeping, Lamia moved silently and freely.

*As the raven I look upon thee in the day and in the night. Always, always there. Always seeing. I am all creatures and all creatures are me. I see everything through their eyes. I am all that is of this earth. My Lord has given me the power to move between all living things. One touch and you are mine and I am you. I shall shatter your mind. Fear me.*

It was during the week that Sally went to London, showing her designer bags to more upmarket stores, when Paul's woodcarvings really took off. The halogen lamp had been an absolute necessity, enabling him to work long into the night. Like some demon barber, he had shorn the locks from chunks of wood in a frenzy of delight. Loving every movement, especially the cutting action of his chisels. He delighted in selecting the right tool for each job with infinite care and breathing in the smell of wood like some heady perfume.

Cracks had appeared in some pieces, as the wood had dried out. But somehow that added to the character of the objects. He hadn't taken Father Willoughby's advice and made matching crosses for him and Sally, but now – along a shelf in the barn – stood a row of carved oak wooden ornaments; a dormouse with a wedge of holey cheese, a pair of clogs and a horse with a decidedly delicate tail. His current project was his most ambitious so far, a head and shoulders bust.

At the moment it could be male or female, it hadn't yet revealed itself. More and more he was feeling that it wasn't he who was creating these objects. It was as if they were there all along, it was just his job to smooth away the wood shavings to reveal what was inside each chunk of wood.

His forages into the forest were almost daily, and always to the fallen oak, loving being able to bring useless pieces of wood back to life in other incarnations. Creating something from almost nothing was as powerful as a drug.

Working under the warm intense light of the halogen lamp, he delicately shaped the crown of the head. There was a smoothness to its high forehead and a natural rise as if that was where the hairline began. As he worked he could see the way the hair would be swept back, forming wings over the ears – even though he hadn't started on the ears yet. He sensed there would be short thick sideburns. So, male it was. For a while he'd wondered if he was subconsciously creating a bust of Sally. He prayed it wasn't an effigy of Helena. Though he doubted it would look like anyone in particular when he'd finished.

Moths were fluttering around the lamp, and then came another sound from the open barn door. He looked, but saw nothing beyond the dazzle of light that encircled him. For a second he felt the total isolation of his position, and the fact that he could be seen so clearly, yet unable to see a thing beyond his spotlight of illumination. Years of training were back in an instant.

His hand tightened around the chisel's handle and he swivelled the lamp on its pivot towards the door. Then he stood, before calmly walking through the barn to the back door. Quietly opening it, he stepped out into the semi darkness. He trod silently, making his way around the side of the barn, keeping close to the walls. Peeping around the corner, the beam from his lamp lit up a tree and the glow of two pairs of eyes became apparent.

As his own eyes adjusted he could make out the shape of a cat, sitting stock still at the base of the tree, while on a branch sat an owl.

'Bloody cat!' He laughed to himself. It was an odd hollow sound in the silence surrounding him. 'Hello Bluebell, if you're looking for Sally, she's not back till tomorrow.'

He'd been putting food down for her as instructed, although this was the first time since Sally left for London that he'd actually seen the cat, even though the food had been duly eaten twice a day.

'So, who's your friend?' He chuckled to himself, as a thought struck him, and he recited the nursery rhyme to his audience. 'The owl and the pussy-cat … didn't they go to sea in a beautiful pea green boat? They took some honey and plenty of money wrapped up in a five-pound note … Hey, how about that? Another memory from when I was a kid. You need to scare the crap out of me more often.'

Unimpressed, Bluebell stood up, turned and strolled away, tail high. As if the show was over, the owl also took flight, spreading its magnificent wings in a silent flapping of feathers, soaring off into the night, vanishing like a ghost.

The following day he finished work and his woodcarving early. With a deliberate and conscious effort, he placed his tools away, left the bust amid its wood shavings and closed the barn door.

Showered and changed, he set about making dinner for Sally's return. Spaghetti bolognaise was something he could do decently. While frying the mince, he checked the time. Sally had texted him just before leaving London. He guessed she would be nearly home now, just hitting the narrow winding lanes.

His head ached suddenly. Not the agonising shooting pains he'd felt on his arrival. They, thank God, hadn't returned. This was just a twinge of pressure, a bit of stress that came with worry.

He concentrated on the food, adding herbs, bringing a pan of water to the boil for the spaghetti. This had been one of Helena's favourite meals. He remembered then, they'd had spaghetti bolognaise the night before the accident. It had been their last supper.

A steel-like band tightened around his head and Paul's thoughts flashed back. He was in his car, following Helena. He saw the tanker hurtle around the bend, and the driver's expression as he fought to control the vehicle. Standing rigid at the cooker, Paul saw with utter clarity Helena's car slamming into the lorry, metal compacting. Then he was running towards the carnage. Her face … dear God, her face. Why couldn't she have died instantly if she'd had to die at all?

He'd cursed the tanker driver. Cursed him for having a cat in his cab – a fact that had come out at the inquest. Cursed him for dragging him away before the whole thing exploded. For years afterwards, he'd wished he'd died with Helena. It was only since meeting Sally that life had become bearable again.

What he thought was the smell of fuel burning turned out to be the mince, baking itself to the bottom of the saucepan. He scraped it off before it was totally ruined.

He put the spaghetti back in the cupboard and reached for rice and chilli flakes instead. Chilli con carne would be good for their supper tonight. Helena had never liked spicy food.

The table was set, and the kitchen filled with a delicious aroma of chilli when Sally came in loaded down with large plastic boxes that held her leather bags. Although she looked tired, there was a huge smile on her face.

He relieved her of the boxes then took her in his arms. 'God, you smell nice,' he said between kisses.

'Oh wow! What a lovely welcome home. I'll have to go away more often.'

'I've missed you,' he said, which wasn't exactly the truth. The fact was his woodwork and office work had occupied him so much he'd barely given Sally a thought.

'And I've missed you,' she said, her eyes sparkling. 'But I've had such a fantastic week. I've negotiated loads of new deals with shops – some really upmarket ones, too.'

'That's wonderful!' He tried to match her excitement, tried to banish Helena's screams from his head which had agonisingly turned to Sally's screams as the minutes had ticked by before she'd arrived home. 'I'm so pleased for you – and proud of you. You deserve it.'

She kissed him again and broke free. 'It's brilliant, isn't it? Anyway, I'll give you all the juicy details in a mo. I need a shower, and am I right in thinking you've cooked? Something smells delish!'

'It's just chilli con carne.'

'Fantastic! Will it wait another ten minutes?'

He forced a smile. 'It can … I can't. Hurry back.'

Sally laughed, and then looking up into his face, threw herself back into his arms and hugged him tightly.

As she showered, Paul took some deep steadying breaths. She was home, all was well. The past was well and truly in the past. He had to let it go.

He uncorked a bottle of rich, fruity burgundy and drank half a glass as he stirred the chilli. Listening to her movements upstairs, he timed the meal perfectly for her returning back down.

She looked like an angel. She'd put on a flowing, ankle length dress, which could have been a nightdress. He hadn't seen it before. He loved the way it moulded itself to her body. It was so light and see-through, presumably a negligee. He wasn't that well up on women's fashions. Helena generally wore pyj– he stopped himself. Sally wore see-through negligees and that's what was important now.

He looked her slowly up and down and gave an appreciative wolf whistle.

She giggled. 'I bought it in Oxford Street. Gorgeous, isn't it?'

He had an urgent desire to feel it – or rather to feel *her*. She felt as good as she looked, and he struggled not to make love to her right then and there on the kitchen table.

But he guessed she was hungry, and besides, the night was young, and they had the rest of their lives together, didn't they?

*Take all the pleasures you have been given. I know you will, as all your kind have always assumed that pleasure is free. Nothing is free. Nothing. You will end up paying for everything. Happiness is a short-lived thing. But my happiness will be their bitter end. I go in the Devil's name.*

When Sally saw the array of wood carvings the following morning, she beamed with delight. Paul tried to see them through her eyes, but only saw the mistakes and the faults that a real craftsman wouldn't have made. He'd done some research online, and waxed the ends, leaving just a small patch at the bases to act as a kind of drain for the moisture to seep out. And he'd varnished them. Nevertheless, he was bemused by her reaction.

'I can't believe this?' she said, picking up each object and examining it. 'I knew you were improving, but this is just amazing.' Then she looked at him and gave him a playful jab. 'Oh, I get it. You've gone out and bought these as a joke.'

'No, not at all,' he answered, taking the carving of the horse from her. 'They aren't that good. Look, its tail is far too thin at the base of its rump, it'll probably snap off. And the clogs, one's bigger than the other – not that they're meant for wearing. I thought you could plant flowers in them or something.'

She continued to look incredulously at them. 'You could sell these. People would pay good money for them.'

He laughed. 'I don't think so.'

'But they would.'

His arm slid around her shoulder. 'I haven't made them to sell. It's just a bit of fun. My way of relaxing, a break from the daily grind.'

'I'm surprised you've had time to do any work. You must have spent hours beavering away in here.'

'Don't worry, nothing's being neglected. They aren't going to fire me for skiving off.'

She shook her head. 'As if! No, I'm just so impressed. Tell you what, we'll take these into the village this afternoon. Juliet, the woman who owns the craft shop and stocks some of my stuff, will absolutely love these.'

'I bet she doesn't!'

'Trust me, Paul, she's going to snap them up.'

'Fifty pence says she doesn't.'

Sally pretended to spit in her hand then they shook on it. 'Right! You're on.'

'Did you really spit?'

She poked him and smiled.


Sally's hand fitted perfectly into his as they strolled through the woods later that day, although she was forever flitting off like some wood nymph, picking wild flowers, examining some strange piece of fungi or beetle.

Paul had been coerced into putting his carvings, bubble wrapped, into a holdall which he dutifully carried, knowing full well that no one in their right mind would want to stock them. This truly was a case of beauty being in the eye of the beholder.

Sally had intended sticking to the path, but Paul was keen to show her his fallen oak first. It was way off the beaten track, and he marvelled at how he'd come across it in the first place.

The sight of the stricken tree stopped Sally in her tracks. She stared at the tangle of roots horribly exposed to the elements. 'Oh, my goodness! How tragic.'

'Isn't it,' he agreed, although he had long since stopped seeing this as a tragedy. Instead he saw it as a perfect source for the raw materials he needed for his carvings. Almost at once he spotted a branch with a knot in the bark that looked curiously like a face. If he cut that piece out and then sawed downwards he could make a kind of picture from it. It was an old face, or maybe it just looked old because of the wrinkles in the bark. A spark of excitement ignited deep within him and he could hardly wait to start working on it.

Sally walked the length of the fallen oak. 'There was a storm the winter before last. We had a sort of freak mini tornado. It must have happened then. Although you'd think it would have been protected from the wind, being in the middle of the forest like this. Diseased, I suppose.'

Paul stooped down, letting his hand smooth over the grooves and cracks of the face in the wood. Closer, it lost some of its impact. Best viewed from afar, he figured … like an oil painting.

'Oh my God!' Sally screamed suddenly, jumping back as if she'd been stung.

'What? What is it?' He ran around the tree to where she stood, hands clasped to her mouth.

She was still backing away. 'Careful! Careful, Paul, there's a snake.'

'A snake. I thought you'd seen a …' he didn't know what he'd thought. Something horrible. But it was just a snake. 'It'll be a grass snake. It won't hurt you.'

'It was an adder,' she argued. 'I saw its zig-zag markings. It's gone under the trunk. Look you can just see its head. It's peeping out at us.'

He crouched down and peered to where Sally was pointing. He couldn't see it at first, the way its brownish-red skin blended in with the forest floor. And then he spotted two eyes watching him with their tell-tale vertical pupils and the V-shaped pattern on the back of its head.

'You're right! How fantastic! God, it's been years since I saw an adder. In fact, I've only ever seen one once before, when I was a kid and Owen wanted to …'

A memory opened up. So vivid it could have been from a moment ago. He could picture himself pointing excitedly. 'Owen look! It's an adder.'

But Owen hadn't shared his excitement. *'Kill it!'* he'd yelled back. *'Kill it! Get a rock, smash it!'*

'No!' he'd cried, horrified that Owen would want to kill anything so beautiful.

'You're chicken!'

'I'm not.'

'Kill it, then!' And Owen had thrust a rock into his hand. 'Go on, prove you ain't chicken, crush its skull in. Go on, kill it!'

'No, why should I? It isn't doing any harm.'

'They're poisonous. Kill it!'

He could picture it now coiling its way through the long grass and all the while Owen yelling *chicken, chicken, Christian is a chicken!*

So, he'd raised his arm, took aim and sent the rock hurtling – deliberately aiming to miss. 'Shit! Missed it! Find me another rock, Owen, quick.'

Owen's freckled face faded into the past again, and Sally's snake recoiled deeper under the fallen tree and out of sight.

She clutched his arm, pulling him away. 'Leave it, Paul, it might come after us.'

'It won't, sweetheart. It'll be terrified of us.' He laughed at her startled expression. 'It won't hurt you – honestly. It's just trying to get away from us.'

She grimaced. 'Do you think there's more?'

'Probably. But it's unlikely you'll ever see another one. Think yourself privileged seeing an adder in the wild.'

She shuddered as she dragged him back in the direction of the path. 'Privileged? That's not how I'd put it! And stop laughing at me.'

# Chapter 10

Juliet, practically fell over herself to snap up his efforts. She was about ten years older than Sally, with wild auburn hair and a smattering of freckles that turned a rather plain face into something slightly cute. Her clothing reminded him of the old hippy style of the seventies, cheese-cloth and sandals. She looked the part of a craft shop owner. Her shop smelled of incense and candles and had the air of an Aladdin's cave with all its handicrafts, treasures and ornaments. The lighting was dim, and the room felt warm and heady.

'They're fabulous, aren't they, Juliet?' Sally raved on, her blue eyes flashing *I told you so* glances every two seconds.

'I love the feel,' said Juliet, smoothing her bejewelled hand over the curves in the wood. 'There's a vibrancy to them. You've captured the essence of the wood, of nature. I love them.'

Paul narrowed his eyes, not sure whether she was for real or maybe high on something. And then it dawned on him. He led Sally to the rear of the shop. 'Is this a cunning plan you two have cooked up to make me feel good?'

'No!' she answered indignantly.

'Yes, you have. You didn't want to lose fifty pence. I'm onto your little game, young lady.'

She groaned. 'Be told, will you. Your stuff is good.'

'You sure she's not just taking the piss, raving on about them?'

'It's her way,' Sally murmured. 'She's a bit weird but that's because she's a witch. And you can wipe that smirk off your face. She's a white witch.' She went back to her friend. 'So, what do you think, Juliet, honestly? If they're crap, say so.'

Juliet was holding the mouse and cheese. 'They're alive! Wonderful. You have a unique style.'

'*Style*? Just how much is Sally paying you?'

'She's not paying me a bean,' Juliet said, levelling her grey eyes at him.

The look she cast him was slightly unnerving. White witch, black witch – any sort of witch made him uneasy. People – even the worst sort, he could handle, but this supernatural shit was disconcerting. Something he could do without. He guessed it stemmed from his childhood. Some fairy story that had scared him.

'But *I'll* pay you,' Juliet continued, bringing his thoughts back to the present. 'If I wrote you a cheque now for fifty, would you be happy?'

'Fifty?' he puzzled.

'All right, sixty.'

'No, no, fifty's fine.' He looked at Sally's beaming face. 'If Sal's happy, I'm happy.'

'And I'd be glad to take anything else off your hands.'

Sally threaded her arm through his. 'See I told you they were good.'

True to her word Juliet wrote him a cheque. He was putting it into his wallet still totally bemused when another customer came in. Juliet greeted him with a kiss. The action endeared her to Paul, making her seem less witch-like. But then his attention switched to the man himself. He was stocky, about his age, shorter, gingery coloured hair going thin on top, and a complexion that was slightly ruddy. It was a face that sent bells ringing in Paul's head.

Sally smiled at the man. 'Hi there! How are you? I've not seen you in a while.'

'Overworked, under-paid. Oh yes, and I bought one of your leather wallets the other week and my money still keeps disappearing out of it.'

Sally laughed, then hauled on Paul's arm. 'Right, now *here's* someone who will definitely speak his mind. Owen, what do you think of these wood carvings?'

*Owen*! No wonder he had looked familiar. No wonder …

It really was Owen, forty years older, a hundred pounds heavier, a few lines and creases, but it was him, all right.

Owen paid him no attention and Paul stared fascinated at seeing his old pal again after so long – especially when he'd just been thinking about him. He'd forgotten how pale his eyes were. They'd been pale blue, now they looked pale grey – the boyish colour washed away. Paul watched him pick up the carving of the horse and had the distinct feeling that he was going to deliberately snap its tail off. He didn't.

'Yeah, not bad,' Owen finally said to Sally. 'Why do you ask?'

'Because my boyfriend made them, and he has no idea how talented he is.'

Paul wondered how long it would take his old pal for the penny to drop. As far as he could remember, the last time they'd set eyes on each other, Owen had been building a bonfire.

'Owen, this is Paul,' Sally introduced him. 'Paul, this is Owen, Juliet's partner.'

'Pleased to meet you, Paul,' Owen said before his eyes narrowed and he really looked at him. 'Paul? Crikes! Not Paul Christian?'

'The very same,' Paul beamed, grabbing Owen's hand and shaking it madly while Owen stood there dumbfounded.

'You know each other?' Sally exclaimed, looking quite stunned.

'Best friends,' Paul said, his grin stretching from ear to ear.

'Were we ever!' Owen roared, throwing his arms around Paul and practically bouncing him up and down on the spot. 'Paul Christian! Paul! My old mate. Where the hell did you go?'

Owen stood, waiting for an answer. Paul didn't even understand the question.

'I came to see you,' Owen babbled on. 'Every week I sat and watched you lying there, tubes coming out of every orifice.'

Sally touched Paul's arm. 'The crash?'

He shook his head.

There was a catch in Owen's throat as if at some time in the past he'd shed a tear or two over his pal. 'I heard you'd woken up after God knows how long but I couldn't get to see you. I'd got chickenpox or some bloody thing. When I finally made it to the hospital, you'd gone. There was never anyone at your house either. I thought you must have died and they'd lied about you waking up.'

'We moved to London,' Paul explained, quite touched that Owen had waited all that time for him to come out of his coma. 'But to be honest it's all such a blur.'

Sally's voice was sharp. 'Am I to gather you were unconscious for a time? Before the crash? After the crash, what? When?'

'What crash?' Owen asked, frowning.

Juliet intervened. 'Shall I tell you what I think? Well, I will, anyway. I think the three of you should get yourselves over to the Crow and Feathers, have a beer and a good old chinwag. It strikes me you have a lot of catching up to do.'

Owen's expression relaxed. 'That sounds a pretty good plan of action.'

'Absolutely!' Paul agreed, catching Sally's eye and seeing the hurt look inside them. 'Sal, fancy a drink?'

Her eyes told him she wanted him alone, so he could explain this traumatic period of his life that she knew nothing about. Paul saw her anger – or was it sadness?

She sort of grimaced. 'Yes, I could do with a drink.'

Following Owen out of the shop, Paul wanted to hold Sally close and explain that there were some things in his life that were too painful to talk about, and other things that he just couldn't remember. But she marched along the pavement, avoiding all of his attempts to take her hand; and Owen strode along in that old swaggering gait he remembered so well. He glanced back, his expression saying that he just couldn't believe his luck at finding Paul again. Like he had come back from the dead.

Owen ordered a round of drinks at the bar while Paul and Sally sat opposite each other at a small table.

'I feel such a fool,' she murmured, her eyes lowered.

'Why do you?'

She took a deep breath. 'Because I'm supposed to be your girlfriend and I know nothing about your past.'

He touched her hand, it was trembling. 'The past is gone. It's the present that matters and our future.'

'But you'd obviously had some major accident, and this is the first I've heard of it.'

'It's not important.'

'It was important to Owen,' she said drawing her hand free. 'There were tears in his eyes. And Owen is such a … well, believe me, he's not the sort to shed tears.'

Owen returned with the drinks, silencing them both. 'I got you a half, is that all right, Sally?'

'It's fine. Thank you.'

Owen drew up a chair, shuffled nearer to Paul, took a swig of beer and wiped the froth from his mouth. 'So where do we start, my old mate? Where do we start?'

Paul took a mouthful of ale, delighted that it actually tasted of something rather than the insipid chemical tang of the lager he was used to. 'This is really good.'

'Locally brewed and it'll knock your socks off,' said Owen. He grinned broadly. 'God, it's bloody good to see you again.'

'So how long is it since you two saw each other?' Sally asked, a sharpness to her voice that Paul didn't recognise.

'I was ten, he was nine, that's right, isn't it?' Owen said. Then he glanced at Sally. 'This poor sod spent his tenth birthday in a coma.'

'A coma!' she gasped, grabbing his hand, almost spilling the drinks. 'How long were you in a coma? What happened, for God's sake?'

'Nine months,' Paul said, knowing this only because his parents had told him, and because by then he could work it out for himself.

'Nine months!' Sally actually swayed, and her hand tightened around his.

'And before you ask me how, what and why, I can't tell you and that's the truth. It's all a blank. A total blank.'

Owen looked steadily at him, his expression guarded, as if working out whether he was telling the truth or not. 'You don't remember being in the woods, and running?'

'Nope!'

'You don't remember tripping and smashing your head on a rock?'

'Nope!'

'You don't remember the ambulance men stretchering you off?'

'Not a damn thing,' Paul said, wishing with all his heart he had the same memory block over the crash that took Helena's life. What he wouldn't give to lose all memory of seeing his wife die.

Owen sat back and took another gulp of ale. Placing his glass back on the table he said, 'So how far back do you remember?'

'Well, I'm fully compos mentis from when I came out of the coma. Fit as a fiddle, in fact. There were no lasting effects. Which was lucky considering the career path I took. But up until then, hardly a thing.'

'But you remembered me,' said Owen. 'Otherwise you wouldn't have recognised me in the shop.'

Paul patted his old pal on the arm. 'The docs did say that things might come back to me in time, and it's since moving back to this area that I've had little flashes of those days and, funnily enough, you've been in every one. So, either something pretty traumatic took place that's trying to piece itself together, or we were a couple of best mates always hanging around together.'

'That's what it was. You and me against the world! So, Paul, my old chum, what line of work did you go into?'

Paul stared down into his beer. 'I went into the Royal Navy, reached the rank of Rear Admiral. Now I'm just biding my time in the Civil Service.'

Owen's pale eyes widened. 'Rear Admiral Christian! Well, I'll be damned! Good on you, my old mate. And now you're stuck behind a desk.'

'Something like that.'

Sally's eyebrows arched. 'Paul, you're being very modest …'

Paul's glance silenced her. He'd love to be able to talk about the things he'd experienced, but working in MI5 wasn't something he spoke about.

They spent the next hour chatting with Paul, learning that Owen ran his own engineering company and that his first wife had died of lung cancer which he admitted was down to her smoking. He'd met Juliet a couple of years ago and while they didn't live together, they lived practically in each other's pockets.

Paul said little about the crash. Only that he'd also been married before and he'd lost his wife in a road smash. He didn't offer any details and Owen didn't ask for any.

It was only as they left the Crow and Feathers and had exchanged mobile numbers and promised to meet up for a meal, that Owen really opened up.

'You know mate, when my first wife died, I thought I'd never get over it, never ever feel any happiness or comfort. I bet you felt that too. Yeah, I thought so,' he added, looking into his eyes without Paul saying a word. 'But then I met Juliet and you met the lovely Sally. And here we are – all happy again.'

'Don't I know it,' Paul said, holding Sally close.

'We're a couple of lucky sods y'know, Paul?

Paul nodded. 'You read my mind. Damn lucky!'

Sally wanted to take a taxi back home. She was still unusually quiet, but Paul felt they needed time to talk. So, as they walked back through the woods he told her all he could remember of the events leading up to him falling into a coma – and even stole himself into telling her how Helena had actually died.

'Oh my God!' she uttered, stopping dead on the forest path and throwing her arms around him. 'You've been through hell.'

'I won't argue with that, and there's been some pretty hairy work situations over the years, which as you know I can't talk about.'

In a way he was glad he'd told her about Helena. He doubted it would ease any pain or banish any dark memories, but at least now she knew. Wanting to lighten the mood, he told her about his early commando training days and the manic Sergeant Johnston who'd bellow at all the cadets, spraying them with spittle, and forcing them to do press ups in the mud.

They spent the rest of the afternoon working – Sally cutting and stitching while he worked on the security arrangements for the Peace Conference. All leave for the Metropolitan Police and emergency services had to be cancelled for the duration of the Conference, and armed military would be on high alert and making their presence known around the Capital. Then there were the overseas intelligence agencies he needed to coordinate with. Without a doubt, this was one hell of a big deal. Lives depended on him and his team getting it right.

That evening, Sally cooked a meal of poached salmon, but an air of melancholy seemed to have settled over her. It was like she was stepping on eggshells. Now she knew his dark and distant past, she seemed afraid of upsetting him. God alone knew why. The worst was over. Because of her he was happy again. She didn't need to pander to him like he was still ill or suffering.

After dinner she went to light the fire. He hadn't told her what he'd seen in the embers and he had no intention of telling her. But he didn't want the fire lit. He told her that instead.

She didn't argue but went upstairs for a bath. She came down wearing a thick heavy dressing gown, fleecy and dark burgundy in colour. He hadn't seen it before and it dwarfed her.

'I didn't realise you were *that* cold,' Paul said as she curled up in the far corner of the sofa.

She pulled the folds of the gown around her. 'I thought a hot bath would warm me, but I feel chilled to the bone. Perhaps I'm coming down with something.'

Paul put down his brandy glass and wrapped his arms around her. He kissed her forehead. 'I'm sorry. I was being selfish. Shall I light it?'

She leant towards him. 'No, I'm warming up now. It's just that it's been a … a strange kind of day.'

'For me, too. I can't believe I've bumped into Owen again, and that he's your friend's partner. Talk about coincidence.'

Her fingers entwined between his. 'I'd never have put you two together.'

'Wouldn't you?'

'No, he's so brash and … well, I think, a bit pushy and opinionated. He's the sort who likes to be top dog. Although he seemed very enamoured with you.'

'I guess there are times when we all get pushy and opinionated.'

'Well yes, but you're never unkind. But I think he could be if he wanted.'

'You probably know him better than I do now. I was just a kid.'

Sally looked steadily at him. 'Was he a bully?'

Paul gave a sharp laugh. 'No, I don't think he bullied me. Can't remember him ever hitting me or anything.'

'There are other ways of bullying.'

'No doubt …' he stopped at the sound of something scraping in the kitchen. 'Sounds like Bluebell is putting in an appearance.'

'Yes, she'll be wanting a fuss.'

On cue, the cat strolled in, head and tail high. Sally patted her thighs, inviting the cat to curl up in her lap as it often did. For once it wasn't interested. It looked at the unlit logs in the grate, then turned its head and looked right at Paul with such a look of contempt on its face that he burst out laughing.

'See that look? You aren't the only one who wants the fire lit, Sal.'

'Poor Bluebell,' Sally said, reaching to pick the cat up.

With a screech it lashed out wildly with its claws, sank its teeth into her hand and shot back through to the kitchen.

Sally screamed, both in shock and in pain. The damn thing had drawn blood.

'What the hell's got into her?' Paul said, jumping to his feet. It was already out of the cat flap. 'It *was* Bluebell, wasn't it? It wasn't some feral imposter?'

Sally dashed into the kitchen and ran her hand under the tap. 'I … I must have startled her with these big baggy sleeves …'

'Here, let me see,' Paul said, taking her hand. There were tears in her eyes, and when he wrapped his arms around her and she fell sobbing against his chest he knew her anguish wasn't just because of the cat's scratches.

When she'd stopped crying, he found some antiseptic and plasters. 'I'll do a field dressing for you,' he said tending to her wounds. 'There … all better.'

She smiled again – a teary kind of smile. 'She's never done that before. I must have frightened her. I'd better go and see if I can find her.'

'Sal, she'll come back when she's ready.'

But Sally was already at the back door. 'Maybe she was hurt, and I touched a sore spot. I'll just see if I can call her in.'

Paul would have preferred for the darn thing to stay out permanently, but it was just like Sally to find a reason for its erratic behaviour. It hadn't looked hurt, the way it padded in and gave him that contemptuous stare.

The cool evening air breezed in through the open door. The nights were drawing in and it was already quite dark outside. Paul didn't actually like the thought of Sally wandering about in the dark on her own. But that was madness. This was her home. She loved everything about this place and it certainly didn't unnerve her. Even so …

He stood in the doorway, gazing out at the shadowy outlines of the barns and trees. He'd missed not doing any wood carving today. He'd liked to have gone out and done some now, but that would hardly have helped the mood of the day. It would wait until tomorrow.

'Sal!' He couldn't see her outline so stepped outside, slightly irritated that she'd vanished completely. 'For God's sake, Sal … I can't see you. Where are you?'

Away from the kitchen light, the garden fell into shadow. He could just imagine her putting her foot down a rabbit hole and breaking her ankle or catching her face on some brambles. She was being totally irrational. Bloody cat. 'Sal! Where are you?'

Silence hummed in his ears. You didn't get silence like this in the city. This was total silence. But then the tiniest little sounds became magnified. Trees rustled. That damn yew tree was scratching at the bedroom window behind him. Something was squeaking in the undergrowth. Far off, he caught the echo of an owl hooting. That beautiful barn owl, he guessed, but the sound felt ominous now, almost unnerving.

He headed down the garden, his feet swishing through the grass. He felt the dampness that came with the onset of autumn. There was a chill in the air. They'd soon be needing the fire lit every evening.

'Sally, where are you?'

He checked the barns and his workshop, but the latches were down. Surely she hadn't gone into the woods looking for the damn cat.

'Sal …' Someone was behind him. Instinct kicked in and he swung around aggressively. She was there. Right in front of him. Wide eyed, white faced. 'Christ, you scared the crap out of me! Sal, don't sneak up on me like that!'

She clung to his arm.

The relief at finding her was more than he cared to analyse, and then he sensed her fear. His wits sharpened. 'What's happened?'

She started leading him back towards the house. 'Nothing. I … nothing, let's go in. Bluebell will be back for her breakfast, I'm sure.'

Paul looked over Sally's head, towards the forest. 'Did you go looking for her in the woods? For Christ's sake, Sal – it's pitch black. What happened, did you lose your bearings?'

'No, I could see the lights from the house,' she said, trying to make him walk faster. 'I was okay.'

'Didn't you hear me shouting after you? I was worried. You just vanished.'

'I'm sorry. Yes, I did hear you. I just didn't want to shout back.'

He looked at her. Her eyes were still wide – wild. 'Why?' he asked calmly.

She was practically dragging him indoors. 'I'll tell you when we're inside. It's so cold out here.'

'It's not *that* cold.' But obviously she felt it, she visibly shuddered as she slammed the kitchen door shut, turned the key and pushed the bolt across.

Paul leant on the kitchen unit, arms folded. Sally bustled about, filling the kettle, spooning coffee into cups. Her hands were trembling. He wrapped his arms around her and grabbed her close. 'Sal, will you please tell me what's frightened you?'

She gave a nervous little laugh. 'Nothing … well, except my own imagination.'

'Well, that can be a pretty powerful source. Go on, what did you imagine?'

'It's stupid,' she said, relaxing a little. 'I thought I saw Bluebell running straight down the garden towards the woods, so I followed her. I didn't find the little madam, but I went in a short way.' She looked at Paul defensively. 'I'm perfectly familiar with the countryside, the dark doesn't scare me.'

'So, what did?' he asked patiently.

'I heard a noise. Just a noise, some animal, I suppose. But it was quite close and while I could hear you shouting for me, I didn't want to shout back in case … in case I alerted it to me. I didn't know what it was. I started to think about that snake. I could imagine one coiling around my ankles. Then two snakes, three …'

'That wouldn't have happened.'

'I know. But for a minute it's what ran through my head. Then I realised the sound was too loud for a snake or a little creature. It was a big sound, like a person – and I froze.'

'Did you see anyone?'

'I thought I did – but just for a second.'

'What did he look like?'

'She …'

He stared at her. 'You saw a woman?'

Sally made another attempt at making coffee. 'It looked like a woman, yes, a very tall woman, but I honestly think it was just my imagination. You know, the trees can look like people at times.'

'So, what exactly did you think you saw?'

She was silent for a while, and then turning her innocent blue eyes on Paul, she said simply, 'A witch. Pointy hat and everything. Paul, I thought I saw a witch.'

An image flicked into his mind. A face hovering over him, contorted with rage. A face that was beyond ugly. A face that snarled and shrieked. *Cat!* Something about a cat. And then the pain – the shooting pain through his skull.

He turned away on the pretext of getting milk from the fridge, not wanting Sally to have something else to fret over. The pain would subside. It had to. But where the hell that vision had come from, he had no idea.

He found some words to fill the void. 'A witch? Like your friend from the shop?'

'No! Like the Wicked Witch of the West, Wizard of Oz type of witch.' She tried to laugh and failed.

'Spooky!' Paul murmured, amazed at how normal he sounded. The pain faded, as did the image, but it left him feeling uneasy. He made his coffee extra strong.

# Chapter 11

The following morning Sally was back to her usual self. Bluebell had strolled in for her breakfast, coiling herself around Sally's ankles as if nothing had happened. He was amazed at how easily Sally could forgive her for lashing out.

Personally, he couldn't wait to feel the wood chisel in his hand again. The fact that rain was hammering down outside only served to give the house a more intimate feel and he felt unusually happy as he worked, with Sally just an arm's length away. Meeting up with Owen again yesterday was the icing on the cake.

Conference calls with foreign security agents were coming in thick and fast as arrangements for the Peace Conference were put in place. The media were working themselves up into a frenzy about it and while he kept his thoughts to himself, he still doubted that it could be achieved successfully. Time would tell.

Sally insisted on making him some lunch before allowing him to disappear down to his workshop. Paul ate it dutifully, feeling that every moment spent eating was time better spent crafting wood.

Finally opening up the barn door and breathing in the scent of freshly carved bark came with a rush of relief and excitement. The vaguely formed oak bust sat blindly on his work bench, held in place with a clamp inlaid with foam so as not to damage the grain. He had no idea whether that was how real wood carvers operated, but it worked for him.

The head was definitely male. The sweep of receding hair indicated, without doubt, that it was male. Paul picked up his narrow gouge, wiping it on a cloth before bringing it close to the chunk of oval shaped wood. From the hairline, he smoothed the blade down over the forehead, shaping the broad expanse of skull; feather-like slithers of wood shavings fell to his feet at he worked.

He found an even more delicate tool for carving the eyes, feathering the tips of eyelashes and eye lids, shaving away just the right amount of wood to reveal the creases and folds of skin around the eyes. If he'd stopped to analyse how he was doing this, he knew he wouldn't have had a clue, but working instinctively, without a plan in mind, his hands, or maybe it was the tools, simply moulded the features, bringing life to a soulless block of wood.

Sally's voice from the doorway made him start. 'Paul, you have a visitor.'

He turned, irritated. He didn't want visitors. But when he saw who was standing beside Sally, his face broke into a huge smile and he strode over to hug his old pal.

'Owen! Good to see you again.'

Owen slapped him on the back. 'You too, my friend. Hope you don't mind me dropping by. Woke up this morning thinking I'd dreamed seeing you again. Just had to get myself over here and double check.'

Paul smiled. 'Yes, I'm here, alive and kicking.'

'And you've turned into a bit of an artist,' he said, wandering over to the work bench. 'Look at this! You went to college to study the craft, then?'

'Lord no. I've only been doing this since moving here.'

Owen whistled. 'Good stuff, mate. You always liked a bit of wood whittling when we were kids. Hey – I bought you a penknife for your birthday.'

'You did indeed, it had a red plastic handle. I remember it. Would you believe, that's one of the few memories I have of those years?'

'Then we've you to thank for his latent skills,' Sally said, slipping her arm through Paul's. 'He's fabulous, naturally gifted. And it's so lovely that he's making use of this old barn – and finding time to relax. If you'd seen how uptight he was when we first met, you'd say he was a different person.'

Paul kissed the top of Sally's head, breathing in the scent of her shampoo. 'I am a different person, Sal. Thanks to you.'

Owen wrapped an arm around his shoulder and gave his old chum a shake. 'What I want is to catch up with the old Paul, see what kind of chap you've turned into. I've given myself a few hours off this afternoon. How about you and me sit down over a pint and *really* catch up.'

'Well, I was just working on this …'

'It'll still be around tomorrow.' He took the chisel from Paul's hand and dropped it onto the workbench.

Paul bit back a sharp retort that these tools needed treating with respect, then realised he needed to get his priorities in order. Owen was right, the bust would still be here tomorrow, and he hadn't seen his old pal in a long, long time.

He dusted sawdust and wood shavings off his clothes. 'You don't mind, do you, Sally?'

She shrugged and gave a funny little smile. 'No. You two boys go off and talk. I've work to do, anyway.'

Owen grinned, that same old familiar grin that Paul remembered so well. 'There! Permission to go out and play. What time does he have to be back, mum?'

Sally took a playful swipe at Owen, then stretched up and kissed Paul. 'See you later.'

Paul closed the barn door with a feeling of reluctance. He could almost hear the bust calling out for him to stay, not leave it locked inside the block of wood. He needed to get the nose and mouth carved, so it could breathe.

He almost laughed at the fanciful notion. There was time enough to work on the carving. Plenty of time.

Owen bought two pints and two double whisky chasers, and they sat in the Crow and Feathers and clinked glasses.

'So, you've given yourself the afternoon off, Owen,' Paul said, swiping foam from his lips. 'I suppose you can when you're running your own company. How's that going, then? Is business good?'

'It's not bad. We've got a pretty hefty order from the MOD, so that will see us through to next summer.'

'Sounds good. What's the company's name?'

Owen told him. Paul recognised the name instantly.

'We make nose cones for warheads, amongst other things,' Owen continued.

Paul breathed deeply. The last thing Owen should be doing was telling anybody what his company was making if it was for the MOD. 'You did sign the Official Secrets Act, didn't you?'

Owen knocked his whisky straight back. 'It's only you I'm telling, and you're no spy, are you?'

'No, I'm not,' Paul answered. 'So how do you feel about being in this line of business?'

'If you want to make money, make bombs! Fair enough, war brings misery, but I didn't start any of the troubles. Besides, if I wasn't doing this, someone else would.'

'True enough,' agreed Paul.

'Anyway, enough about politics,' Owen said, punching his shoulder. 'Do you remember those play fights we had as kids? Jesus, I wouldn't want to mess with you now. They must have fed you well in the Navy. What height are you?'

'Six four, sixteen stone. Have been since the day I joined the Navy.'

'And to think I used to tower over you when we were kids.' Owen laughed. 'Glad you're on my side! Hey, do you remember that old girl, the witch? You used to be shit scared of her.'

Paul stopped, glass half-raised to his mouth. 'The witch?' That ugly hate-filled face was back, clouding his mind.

Owen grinned. 'Yeah, the old hag, lived by the woods. We used to dare each other to knock on her door and then leg it before she came out and turned us into toads or something.'

Paul gulped a mouthful of whisky, thinking it odd that Sally had thought she's seen a witch last night, and now Owen, prattling on about witches. But not in his wildest dreams would he find knocking on an old woman's door then running away, fun, even as a little kid. But what did he know? He'd got no memory of those days. And judging by the look on Owen's face, his old pal wasn't making it up.

'I don't remember that, but the odd thing is, Sally thought she saw a witch in the woods last night.'

Owen raised one eyebrow. 'Well our witch would be dead by now. She must have been eighty when we were kids. Don't know what your Sal thought she saw but it couldn't have been the old dear we used to … er … tease.'

Torment sounded a more apt description, Paul thought, frowning and trying to get this whole tale into perspective. 'We sound like a pair of right little brats. What was she, some poor old woman living alone with a black cat?'

'You remember the cat?' Owen asked, looking down into his pint.

'No. I don't remember a cat, nor the old woman. I'm just surmising. Go on, embarrass me with my misdemeanours.'

Owen slurped on his beer. 'It was just a bit of harmless fun, really. She was, like you say, an old dear living on her own in a cottage by the woods. She did have a black cat. Kids used to call her a witch. Rumours about her went back years. Some people blamed her for poisoning the local church congregation just after the war. She was new around here, foreign, weird. Some reckon she had connections with the Nazis. Others reckoned the cat was her 'familiar', you know, she'd have sex with it. We used to dare each other to peep through her window and see if we could catch them shagging.'

'Jesus!' Paul murmured, shaking his head. 'I don't remember any of this. You sure it was me? I wouldn't find that fun, and unless a bump on the head changed my entire personality, I can't see me doing that.'

'Well you did, matey. In fact, it was a bit of a ritual. We'd play about in the woods, then get bored and hit on her again, just for devilment.'

'Did we ever get caught?'

'We had a few close shaves. I reckon she knew what we thought and played along. She came out in the full regalia one time. Black pointed hat, long black clothes, warts, broomstick, the lot. Christ, we nearly shit ourselves.'

Paul laughed because Owen expected it and took another mouthful of ale. 'I bet we did. But I don't recall any of that. I do remember you building a bonfire, though.'

Owen's eyes met his over the rim of his glass. His voice was softer. 'You remember the bonfire?'

'Yes, I remember you building a bonfire, and I was whittling something from a bit of wood. A cat, I think, or a dog. Do you remember that?'

'I remember,' he said fixing Paul with a sharp look. 'What else do you remember about that day?'

Paul thought back but all he could see was his own hands whittling away at the wood, the penknife with the red inlaid handle, and Owen building a bonfire. 'Nothing really. That was it.'

'You don't remember seeing the bonfire burning?'

Paul shook his head.

'Don't you?' Owen pressed, leaning towards him. 'Are you sure you don't remember something burning in it?'

'No. Should I?'

Owen shrugged. 'I thought you might because that was the day.'

'What day?'

Owen looked steadily at him. 'The day you bashed your brains in.'

Paul rocked in his seat, stunned that the one sparse memory was of that fateful day. Was that why he remembered fragments of it? Like shards of broken glass leading up to it. 'What happened?'

For a good minute Owen sat silently, his gaze switching from the bottom of his whisky glass to Paul sitting opposite. Finally, he said, 'You ran. We got into trouble for lighting a fire in the woods and you ran. You stumbled, hit your head and the rest is history.'

'Simple as that?' Paul murmured. 'Was someone chasing us?'
He nodded.

'Who?'

Owen shrugged. 'Just some passer-by – same bloke that rang
for the ambulance when he saw the state you were in.'

Paul had the distinct feeling that his friend was lying, but about
what precisely he didn't know. 'Did you come in the ambulance
with me?'

More hesitation, then finally Owen shook his head. 'I wasn't
allowed. I came and visited you in hospital though, mate. Time
and again I came and saw you lying there. I thought that maybe
on your birthday you'd wake up. We made a right din that day. All
the kids from class made a special vigil to your bedside. We all sang
Happy Birthday and left presents for you. Then Mrs Bentley, you
remember her? Well she started crying and we all came home again.'

'Mrs Bentley! I'd forgotten her. She was lovely.'

'It was her who told me you'd come out of your coma. But
then I went and caught chicken pox like half the class that month,
and couldn't come to see you. Then you'd gone – empty bed. Went
to your house and it was up for sale and you'd all left. I was sure
you'd died, mate. Positive of it.'

Paul reached across the table and squeezed his old friend's arm.
'No, I didn't die, we moved soon after I got out of hospital. You
go where your parents tell you at that age. Anyway, it's good that
we've found each other again.'

Paul got the beers in and later Owen insisted on getting
another round. They were half cut by the time they left the pub.

'Have you got to get back to work?' Paul asked, as the fresh
air hit him.

'Not especially. Why, got something in mind?'

'Yes, I fancy seeing my old house again.'

Owen looked delighted. 'I'll take you.'

'Great. I wonder if it's changed much?'

'Let's find out.' He turned and began walking with real
purpose.

Paul fell into step and he listened with interest as Owen pointed out various landmarks and related tales about things they'd done.

Eventually one particular street lined with red-bricked cottages sent a twinge of déjà vu through him. He was close to home. He could feel it in his bones.

'Is anything coming any clearer now?' Owen asked.

'Fourth house from the right, yes?' he murmured, knowing he was home.

Owen nodded.

It felt quite strange as they approached his old house with its long front garden. He could picture himself, a scrawny kid in short trousers, racing out of his front door, *'See ya later, mum!'* and her standing in the doorway, *'Back by tea time – and behave!'*

'Number eight, yes?'

'You got it, mate.'

'I remember it. My bedroom was at the back. I'd come out of the front gate and head this way to catch the bus to school or that direction to play in the woods.'

'Dead on, mate.'

Paul smiled and patted his friend's shoulder. 'Thanks for bringing me, Owen. This is just … well, incredible.' He glanced at his watch. 'Anyway, time I was getting home.'

Owen held up a hand. 'I've something else to show you, my old friend. Another little memory jerker. Follow me.' He walked on, towards the woods. Then stopped and looked back at Paul. 'Come on. This should definitely bring back a memory or two.'

Bemused, Paul caught up with him. Owen strode on in silence, his gait so familiar now that he could practically turn back the clock and see his school pal swaggering along, catapult sticking out of his back pocket. *'Well, come on, then. You chicken or what?'*

Cutting through a gap between the cottages opposite, they emerged near another block of houses, detached, more upmarket. The end house was the doctor's house. Paul remembered as clear as day how he'd sat in the stuffy little waiting room, the gas fire pop-popping as it poured out its heat on the old folk coughing and sneezing. He couldn't remember why he was there. A cold probably – or maybe it was a verruca. Yes, he remembered now. He'd had a verruca.

'Doctor Scott's place,' he said as they walked on.

'Right on! Doctor Scott junior is running the practice, now.'

Paul nodded, vaguely remembering the doctor's son as a snooty little kid who always had a cold.

There was a brook to the left and a small humped brick footbridge. 'I used to play here,' he said softly.

'*We* used to play here,' Owen corrected him.

'Didn't we catch newts in a jar?'

'And frogspawn.'

Paul smiled as they walked over the little bridge towards the forest of trees. 'I'm trying to get my bearings here, Owen. This is the same forest that ends up at Sally's place, well *our* place, isn't it?'

'Yup! The village is kind of enclosed by the woods. If you took an aerial photo, you'd see they're in a crescent moon shape.'

They headed along a pathway until the sight of an old grey stone cottage stopped him in his tracks. 'I remember that.'

'And so you damn well should.'

Paul could hardly believe his eyes. He'd forgotten about this place, but now the memories flooded back. It was grey and ancient, a slate roof that he could reach up and touch now. As a kid the cottage had loomed large and foreboding, filling him with dread. Taller now and older, he realised that it still did.

A crow sat hunched up on the apex of the roof, watching them. Hadn't there always been a crow perched there?

'*Bang the door, Paul!*' He could practically feel Owen shoving him. '*Go on, do it now. Give it a good kick, that'll scare the pants off her, if she's wearing any. Go on, then!*'

'It's the witch's house,' Paul murmured, rocking slightly on his heels, the terror of those childhood days hitting him like a hammer. 'God, it gives me the creeps even now.'

Owen's face beamed, reminding Paul so much of the kid that once lived in his skin. 'I thought it would jog your memory.'

'We really believed a witch lived there, didn't we? I used to be terrified. I never wanted to bang on her door you know, mate. I was so scared.' He stopped short in accusing his pal of forcing him into doing it. What was the point?

'Yeah, fun, though. I wonder who lives there now?'

He backed away. 'Don't know, don't care. Mate, I have to get home. It's going to take me an hour to walk back, and if I don't get a move on, it'll be getting dark and there's a fair chance I'll lose my bearings in the woods.'

'But aren't you curious about her? Whether she's still around? She could be. Maybe she was just an ancient-looking sixty-year-old back then, she'd be a real old crone now, bordering ninety but she could still be in there.'

Paul stared at Owen in amazement. He was still a little kid at heart, and one full of devilment at that. 'Are you seriously suggesting we go knocking on some old woman's door, putting the fear of God into her? She'll be ancient for Christ's sake, we'd give her a heart attack.'

'Go on, where's your sense of adventure?'

It was just so ridiculous that Paul could have almost laughed. 'You know what Owen, you haven't changed a bit.'

Owen grinned. 'You neither, mate. You're still chicken.'

With a shake of his head, Paul turned and walked back the way he'd come. Owen came sauntering after him, chuckling to himself in that unique way of his.

Paul halted, turned and waited for Owen to catch up with him. Then slapping an arm around his shoulder, he laughed. 'Are you ever going to grow up?'

'One day, probably,' Owen grinned. 'But not yet.'

# Chapter 12

Paul lay in bed listening to the yew tree tapping at the window pane, then turned his head closer to Sally's.

'What's it saying?' he whispered into her ear.

She lay quietly for a moment. 'Sally Knightly loves Paul Christian.'

'No, it doesn't. It's saying that Paul Christian was a right little shit when he was a kid.'

Sally turned on her pillow to look at him. 'Why on earth would it say that?'

'Because it's true.'

Her hand stroked his chest. 'What did he tell you? Owen, I mean. It has to be him that's reminded you about something you did as a child. You shouldn't take any notice, Paul, I swear that man is a bully. I think he bullied you as a child and if you're not careful he'll be bullying you again. Don't let him get into your head.'

'I don't think so, honey. But you're right about him telling me what I used to get up to.'

Sally leant up on one elbow, her face half illuminated in the moonlight. 'I can't believe you'd do anything bad. You were just kids.'

'Well, I hate to disillusion you, babe, but I was a right little brat. Seems I used to knock on some old woman's door, then do a bunk.'

Sally chuckled. 'Is that all? It's hardly a hanging offence.'

'We tormented her, regularly. We probably made her life hell.'

'He probably put you up to it.'

'Well yes, you're probably right about that, but I could have said no.'

Sally ran her fingers down his cheek. 'Not when you're only eight or nine and your best friend is bigger and older than you.'

'Maybe. It doesn't make me feel good, though.'

She lowered her lips to his. 'Go to sleep, Paul. It was a long time ago. There's nothing you can do about it now.'

He lay awake wondering if maybe there was.

At the first opportunity, he got back to work on the bust. He needed to do the nose. To open up its nostrils so it could breathe. It was a ridiculous notion, but he worked feverishly until he felt the nose draw in its first breath.

'That's better, isn't it, my friend, whoever you are.' He stood back and admired his handiwork. The top half of the bust looked vaguely familiar – the broad forehead and sweep of hair, the strong, straight nose. It felt as if he was working from memory, but the memory of who?

Paul brought life to the eyes next. A light touch of a sharp knife to the blank, open eyes gave outline to the irises and pupils. The bust looked right at him, its creator, and for a whimsical second he thought he heard a faint sigh of satisfaction.

Sally brought him some soup and a crusty roll at some point, then tea and coffee. She said nothing about the bust, in fact she barely glanced at it. She looked at Paul, though, and a frown overshadowed her pretty eyes.

His week was spent mostly in London. With the Peace Conference just a matter of weeks away now he needed to liaise with his department to ensure nothing had been overlooked. Logistics needed working out regarding routes, buildings, sewers, everything needed to be checked, looked at for possible vantage points for would-be snipers and bombers. Putting all the world's leaders into one of the city's best hotels seemed a good option. The idea being that fanatical objectors or terrorists from any one nation would hopefully not try to bomb a hotel that also housed its own leaders. At least that was the theory. Paul guessed there were some people who wouldn't give a damn either way. Security was going to be massive, but the PM and Home Secretary knew they could rely on him. He wouldn't be letting anyone down. His team were the best.

Returning home on the train on Friday evening, Paul's thoughts slipped back to his childhood. Since meeting up with Owen again, and seeing the places where he played as a kid, lots of memories of his life before the coma were returning. Worse was the memory of being made to knock on the old woman's door. He pondered over whether that had any connection to the apparition that occasionally flitted through his head.

Those times had been pretty traumatic to him as a kid. He clearly recalled how his heart had pounded and his legs had felt like jelly as he succumbed to Owen's insistence.

*Go on Paul, peep through the window, what can you see?*

He'd seen darkness.

*Knock the door! Go on, bang on the door.*

He'd knocked the door, loud enough to appease Owen, quietly enough not to disturb anyone inside. At least that had been his intention. But she must have been watching for them because one day the door sprung open. He'd tried to run. Owen was quicker off the mark, sprinting away like a gazelle through the woods.

He'd tried to follow – he could still feel the terror, feel the rubbery sensation of his legs which refused to take him anywhere. Any second now he'd be turned into a toad or something. He knew – he was positive she was casting her spell that moment, that's why his legs wouldn't work. Then suddenly he was sprinting down the lane, yelling at Owen to wait for him.

Paul's eyes shot open. A woman sitting opposite in the train carriage was staring at him and he wondered if he'd actually shouted out loud. Slightly self-conscious, he turned towards the window and watched the countryside flashing by.

As the train neared his station he went to call Sally so she could pick him up, then changed his mind. Instead, once off the train, he walked back towards the *witch's* cottage. This was something he had to do, an attempt to rid himself of the nightmares.

Looking at the old cottage, he shuddered at the sight of the crow perched on the roof. It was ridiculous to be spooked by the sight of a crow. They were in the woods for Christ's sake, crows were everywhere. He hadn't stepped back in time, yet it felt that way. Standing there, staring at the drab grey cottage with its solitary window, there was no quelling the churning in his stomach. But at least Owen wasn't pressurising him into knocking the door. He could easily turn around and go home and no one would be any the wiser.

Or, he could walk down the path, knock on the door and wait to see who answered.

He presumed that, seeing as he was dressed in his London style black overcoat and carrying a briefcase, he probably looked like a salesman or a Jehovah's witness. So even if there was anyone living there now, they might not answer his knock.

The front door was smaller than he remembered, and it had been sanded and repainted. It even had a doorbell. Paul pressed at it.

In the silence that followed he felt the urge to turn and run, imagining the old crone that would, at any second, throw open the door and turn him into a toad.

The door opened, and his knees buckled slightly but for very different reasons. The only thing witch-like about the woman standing there in a tight blue sweater were her bewitching green eyes. She was blonde, buxom and beautiful.

She looked him up and down and then smiled. 'Yes, can I help you?'

Paul's first word caught in his throat, and he gave an awkward little cough before trying again. His explanation sounded stupid and lame as he rambled on about how he used to play here as a child, and how kids thought a witch lived here, and how he and his friend would knock on her door then run away.

Her eyes locked onto his, and she listened patiently before another smile transformed her face into an even greater vision of loveliness.

Paul struggled to continue with his story. '… I wasn't expecting her to still be living here. I imagine she's dead by now. But on the off chance, I wanted to call by and apologise for being such a brat and no doubt making her life hell.'

'Well, I think that's admirable. And I can understand you wanting to ease your guilty conscience.'

Ridiculously, he felt his cheeks redden under her scrutiny. 'No denying that. I do feel pretty bad about it.'

She ran her fingers through her blonde hair, smoothing it back from her bright green eyes. 'Well, you could be in luck. I believe the old lady who lived here before I bought the place is in a nursing home now.'

'God! So, she is still alive? That's incredible! Do you know which nursing home?'

She wrinkled her nose, making her look cute as well as gorgeous. 'I think it's the one just off the main London Road. Oakwoods, I'm pretty sure that's the name. It's on the left just after The Woodman Pub. I'm sure you'd find it easily enough.'

'That's good news. Thank you so much.'

Her voice softened, and she extended her hand. 'You're welcome. And if you feel the need to come knocking on my door again, I hope you don't run away.'

The touch of her hand made him smile and he walked away wondering if she had just made a pass at him.

He walked briskly back through the woods, finding his way easily, then veered off towards the fallen oak to see if the face in the bark still looked like something he could work with. It might just have been his imagination, or he might not even be able to locate it now. To his surprise however, he spotted the face in the tree bark straight away.

Tomorrow he'd be back with some tools. It could make a wall plaque, although he doubted anyone would want such a grisly old face peering down at them.

The aroma of roast chicken wafted from the kitchen when he finally got home. Sally fell into his arms, her happy face upturned to receive kisses, which he gave willingly.

'I've missed you,' she said, linking his arm and drawing him into the living room.

The fire was blazing in the grate and Paul hesitated. The crackling of logs, the glow and heat took him back. But as Sally sat him down and placed a glass of red wine in his hand, he realised his thoughts were drifting much further back than the car crash. His thoughts were back to Owen building a bonfire.

Paul didn't broach the subject of visiting the old woman in the nursing home, until after dinner. He guessed Sally wouldn't be in favour and he didn't want to spoil the atmosphere.

She was eager to tell him about more orders for her bags and, to his surprise, the fact that his wood carvings were selling like hot cakes.

'Juliet rang today. She's sold your clogs to Mr and Mrs Clarke – she does the church flowers; the butcher's wife has been admiring your horse ...'

'Very apt.'

'Oh, don't Paul, our butcher only sells quality meat.'

'Only joking,' Paul assured her, with a smile. 'Go on.'

She cast her eyes upwards, 'Let me see, oh yes, the little mouse and cheese has gone to Mrs Scott, she's the doctor's wife. Juliet asked if you'd drop some more pieces in when you can.'

'There isn't anything, really,' he replied. 'I've just been working on that bust. I've another idea lined up, but I'm not sure it will appeal to anyone.'

Sally began clearing away the plates. 'Well, at least it's nice to know that others appreciate your work.'

'It is, indeed,' he indulged her, although deep down he didn't give a damn whether anybody liked what he did or not. 'Oh, by the way, fancy coming with me on Sunday? I need to visit an old folk's home.'

'Really? Is your mother in a home?'

'No, it's not her.'

'Who then?'

'Well, remember me telling you that as a kid I used to knock on an old woman's door and run away? Well it seems she's still alive and living in a local nursing home.'

Sally's jaw dropped. 'Was this Owen's idea?'

'No. Why would it be?'

'Because it sounds like one of his stupid pranks. Paul, she won't remember you, and if she does you'll put the fear of God into her.'

He squeezed her hand. 'Sal, I need to apologise to her and ...'

'And what?'

He shrugged. 'Nothing. I just need to apologise to her. It's bugging me. It's something I need to do.'

'Is Owen going, too?'

'No. I haven't mentioned this to him.'

'Good,' she said, folding her arms. 'Because if he's involved I want nothing to do with it and I'd suggest you don't either.'

'It's me, just me,' he said, looking hopefully at her. 'It would be friendlier having you along, being a woman – and a gorgeous one at that. How about it?'

'Against my better judgement,' she groaned, moving around the table to sit on his lap. 'And I think it's a mad idea.'

'Thank you.'

'So how did you track her down, anyway?'

He stroked her thigh, loving the fact that she wore such soft, silky skirts, even though the weather was turning colder.

'Well actually, Sal, it's been on my mind, so this afternoon I called by the little cottage where she used to live. Someone else is living there now, and she told me.' For a split second he saw those vivid green eyes sparkling with mischief as she'd told him not to run away if he ever knocked on her door again.

'Oh, I wonder if I know her. What does she look like?'

Careful, Paul, a little voice in his head warned. He chose his words carefully. 'I'd say she's about ten years older than you, fair hair, a bit top-heavy.'

'I probably know her by sight,' shrugged Sally, kissing the tip of his nose before getting back on her feet. 'Still, if it helps you sleep easy I'll come with you. But if she freaks out when she sees you and has a heart attack, I'll blame you!'

*With just one touch, the suggestion has been made. Never knowing, never suspecting that my eyes are upon them. I move silently from cat to rat, bird to snake, I see all as they blunder on into the future. A future I have twisted for them. I lust for the fulfilment of my plans. Their suffering is my joy.*

*Mankind believe they are now their own God, such arrogance, creating such things as only Gods can. With powers to destroy the very world they have been given, and this has blinded them from their sad creator. The more they have progressed the easier it has become to end their days. Now is the time for my Master – my God. Now is the time. Now is the final act.*

Paul was asleep the moment his head touched the pillow and at some point in the night he felt Sally's hand fondling him. He lay on his back, eyes closed, loving the sensations tingling through his loins. His thoughts were straying. In his head it was a certain blonde with green eyes stroking him, the fantasy made him harden and when Sally lowered her head taking him into her mouth it was thick blonde hair that his fingers tangled in as he tried to control the rhythm of her movements. It was almost too much, her tongue, the heat of her mouth and before it was too late he took her by the shoulders and pushed her down onto the bed, covering her body with his, thrusting into her – into the green-eyed blonde.

Sally gasped and for the first time Paul opened his eyes. Startling green eyes full of devilments stared up into his. And in the next instant they were gone, Sally's face looked up at him.

She seemed sleepy and confused, as if he'd just jumped on her out of the blue, and that she hadn't been fondling him for the last ten minutes.

Then she was holding him and writhing in unison with his movements, gasping now with a lust that equalled his own.

It was only later when they were both lying beside each other that Paul felt a twinge of guilt. But it was all in his mind, he told himself. He'd done nothing wrong. He hadn't actually made love to the green-eyed blonde. It was nothing more than a fantasy.

Next morning however, he just knew that Sally was going to make some comment, and he wasn't disappointed. He eventually went down to his workshop with the words *horny beast* and *sex-god* ringing in his ears.

The grass was damp underfoot and a cold grey mist hung over the garden and clouded the treetops. Leaves on skeletal branches had turned to gold and a herringbone pattern of fallen leaves carpeted the grass. He lit the paraffin heater and closed the workshop door behind him. The half-finished bust sat on his work bench, staring right at him. It stopped him in his tracks as he tried to work out who it reminded him of. Maybe he'd figure it out when he'd got the mouth formed. At the moment it looked as if the head had been gagged. From the nose downwards the wood was flat and shapeless apart from natural cracks. Paul took up his chisel and stepped up to the bust.

Forming the mouth was easier than he had anticipated, the slithers of oak just fell away, leaving behind a mouth that was slightly down curved. It had a thin top lip, fuller bottom lip, and a chin that told of arrogance and surety. He was lightly smoothing the head with fine sandpaper when Sally came in with a mug of coffee.

She practically dropped it. 'My God! That's amazing! That's President Howard, isn't it?'

Paul stopped what he was doing, the revelation totally throwing him. And of course, she was right. No wonder it had seemed so familiar to him. Good grief, he thought, the power of the subconscious.

In his own mind it was just the bust of some guy. How the hell it had turned into the President of the USA he had no idea. But it was him all right – every inch a dead ringer.

'Paul, you are so clever. This is utterly brilliant. If you sell this to Juliet, you ought to ask a hundred.'

'No, I'm not selling it,' he answered, without a second thought.

She raised her eyebrows warily. 'You're not thinking of putting it on the mantlepiece, are you?'

He smiled, his thoughts racing. 'No, I think I have something else in mind for it.'

'And that is?'

Paul scratched his head. 'I'm just wondering if the President might like it as a gift when he comes over for the Peace Conference.'

'Knowing him, I think he'd love it!' She threaded her arm through his. 'It really is incredible.'

He had to agree that it was – magical, even. Proper wood sculptors took years to hone their skills. This had come ridiculously easy to him and he couldn't supress a little chuckle of glee. He took the mug of coffee from Sally's hands. 'My work is done. Time for a coffee!'

Before the sun completely set for the day, Paul took the axe down from the wall. As ever he relished the feel of silky smooth ash as he gripped the long handle. And feeling slightly in awe of the cold sharpness of the blade, he took it reverently into the forest.

Finding the fallen oak and the particular knotted piece of bark that had caught his eye earlier, he sized up where the axe would have to fall. He was sweating by the time he'd cut through the branch and severed the desired piece.

Carrying it home, the old cracked and wrinkled face stared accusingly up at him, making him whimsically feel that he was carrying a decapitated head. He stopped for a moment and studied the knotted piece of bark. Was it a witch's face? It was certainly ugly enough.

It was almost dark by the time he neared the edge of the woods and could glimpse the distant lights from their cottage. There were scampering noises around him now as the forest came alive with its nocturnal habitants and he could understand how Sally had got so unnerved the night she thought she'd seen a witch. Determinedly he cast the thought aside. What the hell was the matter with him? He'd got witches on the brain.

Picking his way through the undergrowth, and trying and failing to keep to the track he realised the more eager he was to get home, the slower his progress was becoming. The weight of the axe and the chunk of wood were taking their toll and on more than one occasion he considered leaving the chunk of wood and coming back for it tomorrow. Not the axe, though. He wouldn't be leaving the axe anywhere.

Mustering up his energy he trekked on. His downturned eyes concentrating on the forest floor so he didn't trip, rather than keeping an eye out for old crones in pointed hats.

Finally reaching the rear of his workshop he made a silent resolution not to be hanging about in the woods after dark again. It wasn't that he was afraid, but there were better places to spend the evening.

Placing the chunk of wood onto his workbench next to the President, he hung the axe back onto the wall. Then, switching off the light, he closed the barn door and went indoors to find Sally.

She was up to her eyes in Italian leather and had completely lost track of time. The fact that she hadn't made dinner bugged her.

'Sally, sweetheart, don't beat yourself up about it. I don't expect you to cook for me every evening. I'm perfectly capable. In fact, leave it to me. I'll shout you when dinner's ready.'

Her hair dangled over one eye making her look too cute for words. He gave her a kiss before heading into the kitchen.

He went for something hearty – fat pork sausages, big rustic chips and crusty bread. A rich red wine seemed slightly out of place, but it still tasted good. They sat curled up on the sofa under a blanket, talking until midnight. Later, when Paul made love to Sally, it was her and not some green-eyed vixen lying beneath him.

# Chapter 13

*All is as it should be. It is all in motion and these fools know only what they see.*

Back in London, there were meetings with the Home Secretary and confidential discussions with foreign security officials aligned to every dignitary who'd be at the Peace Conference. Paul needed to know precisely who'd be here, every last person. It was always taxing, liaising with foreign agencies, with them all wanting their own minister or state official taken care of with more sense of importance than the next. So, he was thankful for having a good team working alongside of him as tension heightened.

With work being intense, he was more than happy to get the chance to work from home again. Sally stood behind him massaging his neck and shoulders as he sat at his computer.

'Don't let them get to you, Paul,' she murmured. 'Remember how tense you were when we met? You don't want to get like that again.'

He sighed, her touch melting away the stress of the past week. 'I'm trying not to.'

'Good!' she murmured. 'So, are things starting to fall into place, now?'

'Kind of. Although if you read the news headlines, you'd think we were heading for world war three instead of talking peace.'

'There's a lot at stake, I imagine.'

'Absolutely. Do you realise this is the closest we've ever got to finding a solution to the Middle East and the Korean problems? We've got a real chance of people finally living in harmony if these talks go well. But there's always somebody expecting the worse, thinking it's going to go tits up and it'll escalate into a crisis we can't handle.'

'Let's hope not,' she said, kissing the top of his head before going back to her work.

'Amen to that,' he agreed.

It was mid-afternoon when he finally found some free time to go down to his workshop. The short walk across the damp grass took away the final strands of tension and now the familiar tingle of excitement over the prospect of carving wood took over.

A grey squirrel scampered across his path. It stopped and sat cheekily on its haunches to watch him opening the barn door. Familiar sawdusty smells engulfed him and he breathed them in hungrily.

His first job was to light the heater and get some warmth around the place. Picking up the bust of the President he shook his head in amazement. How the hell had his subconscious allowed him to create something so accurate, let alone finding the skillsets needed? He'd waxed the base, except for a small circle that would serve as a drain for the moisture still in the wood and then varnished it. As far as he could tell, it was life-sized, and definitely far more appealing than the piece of bark he'd acquired last week. He picked that up and stared into the wizened old face. It certainly wasn't an attractive face. The features were too sharp; it offered a cold and calculating stare. Male, he guessed, or a very ugly female. And he hadn't a clue what he was going to do with it.

Maybe if he shaped and smoothed the surrounding wood he could turn it into a wall plaque. Though who in their right mind would want it? Still, it would be a crime not to try and do something with it now he'd severed it from the rest of the tree. He picked up a small sander and decided to give it his best shot.

He worked until early evening when Sally came looking for him. Then again through Saturday morning, working with the barn door open so he and Sally could chat. She'd decided to tidy up her garden and as well as raking up all the fallen leaves, was snipping off dead branches and making a bonfire over by her compost heaps.

'If there's any bits of old wood that you can use, Paul, just take them. But I think it's just rubbish, actually.'

What she was piling into a heap was nothing more than twigs – a lot of twigs, and when she finally put a match to them, it caused quite a blaze.

'You've done a good job with that fire,' Paul remarked, standing in the barn doorway. 'I thought you'd be sending up smoke signals.'

'I probably will be in a minute. Still, there's nobody around to complain.'

Paul glanced back into his workshop, feeling incredibly satisfied with his efforts. The wall plaque was propped up on his workbench, finished. He'd given the surrounding background a kind of jagged edge, although it was sanded as smooth as satin, bringing out the beautiful grain of the oak. By contrast the face in the centre of the oval was pure textured bark. His clever handiwork had brought the features to the fore, so undoubtedly it was a face – not just a vague figment of his imagination.

He still didn't like the face. But despite his personal opinions, it was still a pretty neat piece of wood carving. Maybe Juliet would find a buyer for it, after all.

He'd done enough for one day, so after turning off the heater he closed up the barn and wandered over to lend Sally a hand.

Her eyes widened. 'I don't believe it, there's still daylight and you've stepped away from your carvings. I'm deeply honoured!'

'Cheek!' said Paul, giving her a playful slap on the rear. 'I hope you're not suggesting that I neglect you?'

'Well …' she mused, impishly. 'Anyway, grab a rake or some cutters and make yourself useful.'

There were plenty of bushes and trees to trim down and he enjoyed the physical exertion. The bonfire was crackling as he dragged over another mound of raggedy dead wood. He laid the twigs and bits of branch carefully onto the fire, not wanting to dowse the flames. Sally was half hidden under a buddleia bush, cutting it back as he placed another stumpy bit of branch into the fire.

Instantly streaks of blue-green flame shot up from the embers, scorching the hairs on the back of his hands. Filling his nose with the aroma of what he thought was burnt hair. He jumped back. At the same second, he saw something burning in the heart of the fire – the writhing form of a blazing cat.

'Christ!' he yelled, kicking at the burning wood, scattering bits of smouldering and blazing wood in all directions. He picked up a watering can full of rainwater and threw it over the remnants of the fire.

Sally came racing over, fear in her face. 'Paul what is it, what's wrong?'

'Stay back. Don't come any closer!' He leapt over the flames barring her way. She didn't want to see this. Grabbing a stick, he frantically scraped through the fire, where the hell was it? Not that it could have survived. But where the hell was it?'

'Paul, what's the matter? Tell me!' she cried in distress.

He kept on jabbing at the blackened mess of sludge and charcoal. 'Go in, Sally, just go in.'

'I'm not going anywhere until you tell me what's wrong.' She clung onto his arm, trying to stem his desperate probing among the fire's remains.

It wasn't there. Confused, he examined the bits of bonfire he'd scattered around which were still burning. There was nothing but wood, just old smouldering wood. Slowly he sank down onto his haunches, so thankful that Bluebell hadn't burnt to death. But to his horror, he suddenly remembered another cat, long ago, that did.

He lied. Unwilling to let Sally even imagine Bluebell in the flames, let alone admit to what he'd just remembered from his past, Paul lied to her.

'I thought I saw a hedgehog in the fire,' he said, wiping a film of sweat from his face. 'I'm sorry I panicked. It was nothing, but just for a minute I thought it was a hedgehog.'

Sally put her arms around him. 'God, Paul, you risked burning yourself for a little hedgehog. You're such a hero ... crazy, but still a hero.'

Some hero. What kind of hero burns a cat on a bonfire?

To top off a perfect day, Sally received a phone call from Juliet later that afternoon telling her that Mrs Scott, the doctor's wife had been found dead in her home. She'd fallen down the stairs and broken her neck.

Sally sat with Bluebell on her lap and cried.

Paul made a phone call of his own. Owen sounded subdued and Paul guessed that news of the doctor's wife had affected him badly, too. In a way he felt quite guilty in adding to his troubles.

'Can you get out for half an hour?' Paul asked him. 'Meet me at the Crow and Feathers around seven?'

'Well, I guess so. Mind you, the atmosphere over there is going to be a bit grim, what with the news. It's pretty ghastly what's happened to the doctor's wife.'

'Yes, I know. It's upset Sally badly, but that's not what I wanted to talk to you about. Seven, yes?'

Owen sounded puzzled, but agreed. 'Okay, see you there.'

He borrowed Sally's car, glad she didn't want to go with him. He needed to get the truth from Owen.

There was no sign of Owen at the Crow and Feathers when Paul arrived, so he got the drinks in, sticking to a coke for himself.

Owen had been right about the atmosphere. A dozen or so people were drinking, and everyone was long faced and speaking with quiet respect for the doctor's wife.

Paul raised a hand as Owen came in. He acknowledged Paul but stopped to speak quietly to a few of the regulars before coming over. Paul watched him, trying to remember more from his childhood. It was always him and Owen. He couldn't remember any other friends he hung out with.

Shaking his head sadly, Owen made his way over to Paul. 'Nasty do that. And they have two kids at boarding school. What a damn shame, but by God she could be a snooty cow at times.'

Paul didn't answer, but took another gulp of his drink.

Owen took a mouthful of ale. 'Anyway, mate, what did you want to talk to me about?'

Paul toyed with his glass. With his eyes lowered he asked, 'What kind of kid was I – before the coma?'

'Well, I wasn't expecting that.' A bemused expression formed on Owen's face and he rubbed his chin. 'Well, you were just a normal kid. We'd climb trees, scuff our knees, that sort of thing.'

'Scare old ladies,' Paul reminded him.

'Not really, she scared us more than we scared her.'

'So, what else did we get up to? Did we go scrumping apples or raiding birds' nests for eggs?'

'I guess we did.'

'Throw cats onto blazing fires?'

Owen's face dropped, and the ruddiness paled from his cheeks.

'Is that what we did, torture animals?'

'Keep your voice down, will you?'

Paul leant towards him, noticing a fine sheen of sweat on Owen's upper lip. 'Is that what we got up to?'

Owen took another gulp of ale. Placing his glass carefully down before answering. 'We didn't make a habit of it. And besides I don't think you meant to, not really. It was an accident.'

'Me!' Deep down he assumed Owen had done it, if anyone had. The thought that *he* had done such a thing was abhorrent. But he could hear its agonised screeching, it filled his head. He could picture it struggling in the flames, terrified, burning – burning to death. He could even smell it.

He put his head in his hands. 'Jesus!'

'It was a bloody accident! Keep your hair on, you never meant to kill her bloody cat.'

Paul looked slowly up. 'Whose cat was it?'

Owen shrugged, looking guilty. 'Hers! The old woman ... the witch.'

'Great! Not only did we torment the old dear, we killed her pet. I hope to God she never found out ...' Owen lowered his eyes, avoiding Paul's gaze. 'She did, didn't she?'

Owen was quickly on the defensive. 'Well, she got her revenge. So, don't go feeling too bad about it.'

His head was beginning to ache. 'What do you mean?'

Owen looked steadily at him. 'Well, the witch put you in a coma for nine sodding months, didn't she!'

That night as he lay in bed, things were coming into focus. He remembered whittling a bit of wood while Owen had built a bonfire. And he had a clear recollection of a cat burning in the flames, and that smell – the stench of burning fur. Owen had supplied all the missing data so that he could visualise it perfectly in all its gory detail.

He'd explained that earlier that day – the day he'd fallen into a coma – they'd been tormenting the old woman, knocking her door, running away. But she must have seen them coming and when they knocked the next time she leapt out, scaring the pants off them.

Owen had described her as a hag, a real old crone, warts and all. She'd come out ranting and raving and given Owen a sharp poke with the end of her broomstick.

Paul was pretty certain that had been poetic license. A long-handled brush maybe, but not a broomstick. Owen said they'd raced off into the woods and hidden, but she'd come searching for them, looking, according to Owen, every inch a witch. By now she'd acquired a pointed hat and long black clothes, and was as ugly as sin.

Paul had listened, imagining that if it had happened as Owen said, he would have been one terrified little boy.

Eventually, the old dear had given up looking from them, and later when the excitement had died down, Owen built a bonfire while he'd sat whittling. Owen thought he'd been carving a cat and they'd thought it funny when a black cat came prowling through the woods.

'It's hers! It's the witch's cat,' Owen had said.

Paul had coaxed it over and it had come right up to him. But as he went to stroke it, it had sunk its teeth into his hand and clung on, fangs and nails embedded deeply into his arm. According to Owen, he'd leapt about trying to shake the cat off and somehow it had ended up on the bonfire.

It must have been an accident. Unless he'd had a total personality change, never in a million years would he chuck an animal onto a fire deliberately.

Paul had listened in silent disbelief, hoping he hadn't been persuaded to throw the cat onto the fire. He could imagine Owen yelling at him to do just that.

*'Burn it, Paul. Burn the witch's cat! Go on!'*

He'd listened wordlessly to what happened next. It seemed that the old dear had appeared from nowhere. She was just there, suddenly shrieking through the smoke. They'd run like hell in opposite directions. The old woman had picked on him to chase. He was found later, unconscious with a massive head injury.

Sally's hand on his chest brought him back to reality.

'Sorry, didn't mean to wake you,' she murmured.

'I'm not asleep. Just lying here, thinking.'

'Nice thoughts?'

'Not really,' he admitted, but wouldn't be drawn further. 'What are you doing tomorrow, Sal?'

'Just the usual, cutting, stitching. Why?'

'I'm going to visit the old dear in the care home. I'm hoping you'll come with me.'

'The one you and Owen thought was a witch?'

'Yes, that one.'

She groaned softly. 'Are you sure that's a good idea?'

He lay there for a while, thinking. 'Probably not.'

# Chapter 14

*Hidden in full view, I see and hear everything. These puppets - I like to make them dance. They amuse me with their naivety, under some illusion that they can be forgiven for their sins. This is not the place to come and be forgiven. My God is Satan, who never forgives.*

Oakwoods Rest Home was a big old house with a modern extension built on the side. Through wide windows he could see people shuffling about.

Paul felt a twang of unease. He wanted to say sorry, yet deep down it was as if he was apologising for the actions of another person.

Sally linked his arm. 'You're very quiet.'

He nodded.

A woman in a green uniform smiled. 'Hello there, Can I help you at all? There was an Irish lilt to her voice.

Good morning,' said Paul. 'I wondered if it would be possible to see one of your residents. My name's Paul Christian, I grew up around here and I'm trying to catch up with people I used to know. There was one elderly woman who ... who was really kind to me when I was a kid.' A blatant lie, but she was hardly going to let him in if he admitted killing her cat. 'I thought she'd have passed away long ago, but I've been told she's still alive and living here.'

'What's her name?'

'Well, there's the problem. I don't actually know. You don't ask names when you're just a kid. She used to live in the little cottage on the edge of the woods.'

'Oakwoods,' Sally offered. 'Just a couple of miles down the road ...'

'Sounds a bit vague, doesn't it?' Paul added apologetically.

'Do you mean Petronella?' asked the nurse looking pleased with herself.

'Who?'

'Petronella Kytella. She used to live on the edge of Oakwoods.'

'Well, possibly.'

'A Polish lady, according to papers found in her cottage. She migrated here from Germany at the end of the war. I'm sure it's Petronella you're after.'

'How can you be sure?'

'By your description, dear. An elderly lady who lived in a cottage near Oakwoods. There's no one else here that fits that description. So, if you're sure she's a resident here now, it's got to be her.'

Paul glanced at Sally, she looked a lot happier than he felt.

The woman checked her computer. 'She's been here now, let me see ... Ah, it'll be eighteen years this January. Seems a health visitor called on her by chance one particularly bitter cold January and found her in a state of semi consciousness. They had to break in. She wasn't on the council's books. Heaven knows how she was missed. And goodness knows how many years of benefits she was due. But there you go. Some people fight tooth and nail for every penny the State might offer and then there are others who just muddle by without asking a soul for assistance.'

'And she's been here ever since?' asked Paul. 'For the last eighteen years?'

'That's the long and the short of it,' the nurse nodded. 'Our longest standing resident, and possibly the oldest. The Council sold her cottage, which pays for her care costs here, and of course, she gets a pension now. Not that she spends any of it.'

'Why's that?'

She sighed and got up from her desk. 'We'll go and see her, shall we? Then you'll see what I mean.'

They followed her to a locked inner door. She tapped in a code and turned a lock. As the smells of urine and bleach hit them, he and Sally exchanged glances.

'How old was Petronella when you last saw her?' the nurse asked, as she walked ahead in her sensible flat shoes.

'I've no idea. As a kid I thought she was about a hundred, then. Obviously not! She must only have been in her sixties.'

A stooped old chap in a dressing gown and slippers came shuffling along the corridor. His watery eyes looked vague and distant.

'You're not to walk too far today now, Edward,' the nurse said cheerfully, wagging her finger at him.

He mumbled something indecipherable and shuffled on towards the locked door.

The nurse glanced back at Paul and Sally. 'The residents in this part of the home have extra special needs. Most are suffering from acute dementia and mental problems, sadly.'

At the end of the corridor there was a lounge filled with plastic covered armchairs all set out in regimented rows. Most were occupied with the sagging wrinkled aged, some of whom were drooped in sleep; one old woman was chanting, another shuffling about picking up specks of fluff from anyone and anything. There were carers tending to various residents, holding beakers to thin wrinkled mouths, dabbing up the spills with tissues.

Sally's hand slid into his and gripped it tightly.

'Petronella has her own little corner by the window,' said the nurse brightly, veering towards the far corner where a wide window looked out over the gardens.

Paul spotted her immediately. She sat, bent almost double, crumpled into a blue plastic armchair. She looked about a hundred and ninety. She was wearing some kind of flowery frock, a thick cardigan, saggy thick tights and slippers that her gnarled old feet were barely into.

Her head was drooped onto her flat chest so that only the top of her head – with her thinning grey hair, was visible. Her hands were limp in her lap – old liver-spotted hands with thick fingernails that badly needed trimming.

The nurse stooped down beside her chair and gently stroked her old wizened hands. 'Petronella ... Petronella, wake up, darling, you have visitors.'

There was no response. The nurse smiled sadly up at them, still patting and stroking the old hand. 'She's like this most days, I'm afraid. In fact, to be honest, she's been like this ever since I came here. It's so tragic. You'd think when they reach this stage ...' her voice trailed away. Paul guessed what she was thinking. That if it wasn't against the law, there was definitely some argument in favour of euthanasia.

'She is ...' he whispered the words. '... still breathing?'

'Oh Lord above, yes. Her pulse is strong as an ox. It's just her mind. She's away with the fairies. I'll get you a chair and you can sit and talk to her. Sometimes we think she hears us.'

'No, I don't need a chair,' Paul said, turning to Sally. 'Would you mind waiting in the reception, Sal? I just want to talk to her about, well you know, when I was a kid. Please?'

Sally was reluctant to leave his side and he was grateful to the nurse for suggesting that Sally might like a cup of tea while she was waiting.

'If you're sure, Paul.'

'Yes, I'll only be a few minutes.'

'Come along with me, my dear, A nice cuppa ... just what the doctor ordered.'

Sally reluctantly followed. The nurse glanced back to Paul. 'Just wave at me through the glass panel when you're finished and I'll let you out.'

'No need,' he answered. 'I noted the code number."

She raised her eyebrows. 'Did you indeed? Well, good luck!'

Paul waited until they were gone then knelt on one knee beside Petronella. He touched her hand, her skin seemed paper-thin. The smell of age filled his nostrils, that and the smell of sweat and bad breath; and another smell, like the faint waft of burnt hair.

'Petronella … You won't remember me. I used to play in the woods, near your cottage. Must be around forty years ago now.' He waited, hoping for some response. 'I just wanted to say sorry, for tormenting you. I was a little horror, used to knock your door and run away.'

He watched her as he spoke, looking for any sign that she could hear him and understand what he was saying. But nothing flinched, not a muscle in her old sinewy hand, not a change to her breathing, nothing.

'There's something else.' His voice became a whisper. 'Something I thought you should know. Your cat accidentally died in a bonfire that my friend and I made. I'm not sure how it happened, but it did. And I'm truly sorry.'

Again, there was no sign of life – except for the tiniest movement of her head.

'You might remember chasing me. I fell and banged my head. I was in a coma for months afterwards. I'm all right now. Although I daresay you wouldn't mind if I'd stayed comatose for life after what happened.'

Paul tried to see her face, but her thin hair was hanging over it. He gently lifted a strand, so that he could see something of her features. Her cheeks were sallow, grey-white skin like old pastry; wrinkle sagging over wrinkle. Her nose was big and ugly and hooked. It didn't seem fair that any woman of any age should have to bear a nose like that. She had warts, just as Owen had said. Her eyes were closed, the eyelids loose and sagging. He let the hair fall back over her face and got to his feet. It was as much as he could do.

He turned as the old dear who was picking up specks of dust plucked at his elbow. He smiled, and she shuffled away, still picking and plucking.

'Goodbye, Petronella,' Paul said as he walked a few steps. He stopped, needing to take one final look at what, as a kid, he'd thought was a witch. She wasn't so frightening now, just a frail old lady.

He glanced back at her and shock made him reel. Her head was up, and she was staring straight at him. Dark rimmed eyes fixed on his. There was no colour in her irises.

And no forgiveness either.

It was a look that drained the life out of him, making him want to run, to get away before she could cast a spell to shrivel him up. And the smell of burnt hair was worse.

Paul kept on walking. He knew he ought to go back, to repeat everything he'd just said now that she was awake, but irrational fear had gripped him. Something he hadn't felt since he was a kid. He strode down the corridor towards the locked door. It was just like before, knock her door then run. Damn it, he was doing exactly what he'd done as a kid. He was still tormenting her.

He quickened his step, overtaking the shuffling old man still on his circuit to nowhere. The smell seemed to be following him. Tapping in the first two numbers of the code, he felt the sensation of someone breathing down his neck. He jabbed the last two numbers in, but the door stayed shut. His temperature shot up, his neck and face growing redder as he glanced over his shoulder, expecting it to be her. To his infinite relief he saw it was just the old man, not Petronella.

He punched in the numbers again, annoyed with getting them the wrong way around. The door opened, and the shuffling man tried to follow him out.

'Sorry, my friend,' Paul said, truly sorry that the old guy was stuck in here with Petronella. 'I'm afraid you can't come out.'

He felt bad about closing the door in the old chap's face, but relieved that Petronella was on the other side.

Sally was initially smiling to herself when Paul made his way back to the reception, but then her face fell when she saw her lover's expression. 'Paul, are you okay?'

'Yes, fine.'

'Any luck, dear?' asked the nurse from behind her desk.

'No, nothing,' Paul lied. 'I don't think she even knew I was there.'

The nurse smiled sympathetically. 'I didn't think you'd have any joy. But still, you tried.'

Paul linked Sally's arm, eager to be out. The feeling of wanting to flee was totally against his nature, fight or flight; and he wasn't used to the flight syndrome. And as for the burning smell, it was like black molasses, clogging his nostrils. He needed to get away from here, it had been a bad idea. Nothing felt right about that woman. He particularly didn't like the unnerving effect she was having on him.

'Paul,' the nurse called after him. 'If we have any kind of news on Petronella, I'll ring you. Sally has given me your phone number. It's nice that Petronella has someone after all this time. I can't remember when she last had a visitor.'

In the car Sally turned to him. 'Okay, what happened? You don't look at all happy.'

'I'm far from happy, but it's hard to explain. Just drive, Sal. Let's get away from here.'

She turned the ignition and steered the car back onto the main road.

He let his eyes close, leaning his head back on the rest, relieved that the stench of burnt hair was fading.

'I wish you'd tell me what went on.'

He sighed. 'There's nothing much to tell. I said what I wanted to say. I even held her hand, but there wasn't even a flicker of reaction. She was lost in her own little world. Then when I was going, I glanced back for a last look at her, and she was sitting bolt upright, glaring after me with a look of absolute hate on her face.'

'Didn't you go back and speak to her?'

'Sal, I've faced some pretty scary characters in my time, but Petronella is one of a kind. She's weird. In fact, this whole situation is weird and I'm struggling to get my head around it. There's something not right going on that I can't quite put my finger on.'

Sally glanced at him. 'I'm beginning to wish you'd never met up with Owen again.'

'It's not Owen who's the problem here, Sal, it's Petronella Kytella.'

The woman despised him. He couldn't blame her, he'd killed her cat – so it would seem, she'd probably wanted to murder him at the time.

As they drove on, a thought slowly occurred to him.

Maybe he hadn't just fallen and cracked his head on a rock when he was a kid. Maybe Petronella Kytella had deliberately caved his skull in.

# Chapter 15

*Playing with their minds is a joy. Playing with their bodies is also my release.*

For most of the following week Paul worked back in his London office, liaising with his immediate superior, Director General Daniel Rake, and the top men within his team; Desmond Fitzpatrick and Alistair Brooke – all good men who he worked well with and trusted.

His office was on the third floor of Thames House, a Grade II listed building bought by the Government in John Major's time at No. 10. After losing Helena and selling their house, he'd rented a flat on the far side of Lambeth Bridge. Until meeting Sally, the office had been his second home.

Beginning a new life with her was nothing short of a miracle in his eyes. He never expected to find love and happiness again and he counted himself blessed that she'd come into his life. Right now, however, he was glad to be at work. He needed the discipline that his job imposed to stop himself thinking about the balls-up he'd made of visiting Petronella Kytella.

He arrived back at the cottage the following Friday afternoon. There was no sign of Sally or her car but he did come across a note left on the kitchen worktop.

*Gone Shopping, love you xxx*

He changed out of his suit, swapping pinstripe for denim. The weather had turned quite cold, so he added a fleece to his woodworking attire.

As ever, heading down to his workshop banished every other thought from his head. Problems melted away and he was eager again to feel the wood and tools in his hands, knowing they would provide tranquillity, as if the simple action of wood carving was putting everything into perspective.

Unlatching the door, he breathed in the rich woody smells. An involuntary smile moved his lips as he took the axe from the wall. A stroll out into the forest for a new piece of wood was required.

The trees were losing much of their foliage as autumn set in. Underfoot, a thick carpet of mulched leaves scrunched under each step. Reaching the uprooted oak, a variety of sections had distinct possibilities. He was just considering cutting off another sizeable piece to make another bust, when a more twisted piece of branch caught his eye.

It was angled and rough with smaller twig-like branches as off-shoots. Its form reminded Paul of driftwood, a curious tangle of curves; and while he hadn't a clue what to make of it, there was something so fascinating about it. He viewed it from all angles before deciding where to wield his axe.

It was less than two feet long when he carried his prize back home, twisted and misshapen, but he loved it.

Sally still wasn't back, and he was glad to have some time to get acquainted with his raw material. His hands smoothed over the contours and textures. It would be a horizontal piece of work – whatever it turned out to be, even if it was just a piece of abstract rubbish. He couldn't call it art. But it would be horizontal, reclining. And it would need only the most delicate of tools, the narrowest of chisels.

He reached across to his rows of carving utensils, selecting the tool like a surgeon about to perform a delicate operation.

He held the blade to the bark, sensing where the first cut should be, but before steel touched grain, the barn door opened and Sally breezed in. Her arms were around his neck in an instant, and he had to hold the chisel away in case it caught her.

He returned her kisses, determined that she wouldn't even for a second sense his irritation at being disturbed.

'Oh, I've missed you so much!' she declared.

Paul kissed her again, feeling a certain unexpected tingling in his loins. 'I've missed you too, sweetheart.' He placed the chisel back on the rack, aware suddenly that there were more pressing needs to fulfil than carving up a piece of old wood.

'Is everything going okay at work? Or aren't I allowed to ask?'

'It's all going to plan,' Paul said, turning off his heater and leading her out of the barn. 'But right now, my plans are to get you up into that bedroom.'

She gave a little squeal of delight and half skipped – half ran across the lawn back to the kitchen door. Paul gave chase, excitement rising like a fire within him. In the kitchen he kicked the back door shut behind them and when Sally turned to look at him he saw a flash of nervousness in her eyes. It fuelled his ardour even more, stirring up a whole wave of lurid images in his head. He'd no idea where the fantasies were springing from. Certainly not from anything he'd ever done, not even from films, yet flashes of naked bodies darted through his mind, and his body felt on fire.

The desire was too fierce to take Sally upstairs. Instead, he swept her shopping off the table, ignoring her protests that there were breakables in her bags, and backed her up against the edge of the table. He unbuttoned her coat and dragged her jeans down without undoing them, his body straining against his own clothing for release.

'Paul!' Sally murmured against his mouth, half protesting, while at the same time wriggling out of her trousers and fumbling with his buckle and zip.

He pushed her back onto the table, her jeans and knickers dangling from one leg as he moved between her thighs and pressed himself aggressively into her. She cried out, but he didn't ease up. Instead, he turned her over, face down on the table and took her again.

His passion was spent greedily, and as quickly as his desire had erupted, it waned away to nothing, leaving him feeling self-conscious, and something else … something indefinable – *used* almost, even though he'd been the aggressor.

Bluebell had tangled herself around his legs, and he nudged her away as he eased Sally gently to her feet. He felt he ought to apologise, this wasn't his way, but she smiled and breathed a long, happy sigh.

'Paul Christian, I've said it before and I'll say it again – you'll have to go away more often!'

He closed his eyes, exhausted suddenly, needing to rest.

Sally kissed him. 'I think we could both do with a drink. Red?'

He would have preferred to go up to bed, but he nodded and then noticed Bluebell sitting in the corner of the kitchen, her wide unblinking eyes fixed on him like a Mother Superior in a nunnery. In a flash she was gone, out through the cat flap, taking her high feline morals with her.

When he and Sally did finally go to bed, he slept far deeper than normal, his body feeling unusually drained. Ruefully, he realised that he wasn't twenty-one any more.

By the following afternoon, the carving was half formed. It turned out to be a woman, lying prostrate, her back arched, her arms raised, and her head turned aside as if the desire was too much and she was forced to turn away. Her lower limbs were still encased inside the rough wood, waiting to be revealed.

As he worked, he realised that this, more than any piece so far, was playing on his emotions. He didn't usually consider himself to have an overly high sex drive, but as he worked, there was a constant feeling of horniness. Not particularly for Sally, just simply for the act of sex itself. And the more he handled the carving, the more his imagination wandered. Explicit images flashed through his head. Not the sort of fantasy he'd want to share with Sally. These were flashes of naked bodies tied up, raped; totally unpleasant thoughts that kept on coming no matter how he tried to think of other things – as if they had a mind of their own.

The face of the carving was still a mystery to him. Maybe he would start work on that next, or most likely he would begin to form the intimate area of her pelvis and her legs. But for now, he needed to stop.

Looking at her semi nakedness, it seemed wrong to leave her so exposed, and so he found a cloth and covered her. Shutting up the barn, he wasn't sure which of his basic needs required attention first.

There was a smell of fog in the air and a cold mist had settled over the garden. The kitchen lights were on, although there was no sign of Sally. Maybe he would make dinner tonight – afterwards.

She wasn't downstairs, and Paul went up the narrow staircase and into the bathroom, needing to freshen up. 'Hi Sal, you up here?'

There was no answer. Drying his hands, Paul headed for their bedroom but even before going through the door, he could smell the fragrance of scented candles, and saw the flickering glow from the darkened bedroom.

'Sally …'

She was lying naked on the bed, hair splayed across the pillow, her arms above her head, posed almost like the wood carving.

Her eyes sparked in the orange glow of candlelight, full of devilment. Eagerly, Paul fumbled with his shirt buttons, anxious to get out of his clothing. To feel her skin against his.

As he went to lie beside her, her legs parted, and she raised her hips towards him, her fingers tangling in his hair, forcing his head down towards her groin. He eagerly obliged, slightly shocked that his little Sally could be such a dirty little minx when she wanted to be. He was surprised too by her strength, this was a side of her he hadn't seen before, and by God he liked it.

She gripped his hair, controlling his movements, forcing and grinding herself against his face. She orgasmed over and over, then pulling him up she wrapped her legs around his back, locking him into her.

Having satisfied herself in that position, she pushed him onto his back and straddled him, riding him until there was no stopping the inevitable. Finally, Sally flopped her face down onto the pillow, gasping for breath.

Paul lay for a while, not quite sure what had hit him, then turned onto his side and stroked her back. 'Where did that come from?'

She turned her head a little, but her eyes were closed. 'I need to sleep.'

He kissed her spine, between her shoulder-blades. 'Sleep then, my darling. I'll make us some dinner for later.'

She didn't answer.

Sally slept for a good two hours then staggered drowsily down in her fleecy dressing gown and slippers. 'I'm sorry, is dinner ruined?'

Paul had been on his computer, working. He logged out, stood up and kissed her. 'No, it's fine. I can just warm it through. Are you okay?'

She yawned. 'Sleepy.'

He walked her through to the lounge and sat her on the sofa. 'Relax and take it easy. Glass of wine?'

As soon as he asked, he wondered whether she'd been hitting the bottle that afternoon. It would explain a few things. Not that he was complaining.

She wrinkled her nose. 'Cup of tea would be nice.'

'Coming up.'

It was easy enough to re-heat the chicken and vegetable curry that he'd made. He brought it through to the lounge on trays. They were both ravenous and conversation took a back seat as they devoured the lot.

'How are the orders going?' Paul asked her when they'd finally finished eating.

'Good,' she nodded. 'The Covent Garden boutique have sent in a repeat order, which is brilliant. I've whipped up a few random wallets and purses, too. Oh ... and I rang Juliet today to see if she wanted them for her shop, and she was really off.'

'Off?' Paul mused, taking their empty plates through to the kitchen.

'Yes. Really quiet, which isn't like Juliet at all. She said okay to stocking my wallets and stuff, but she sounded weird. You know, not chatty – sort of sad.'

'We all have off days, Sal.'

'Yes, I'm sure she's okay. Anyway, I'll be seeing her on Monday at the funeral. Will you come with me, Paul? I know you didn't know the doctor's wife, but most of the village will be going.'

'I guess so. It'll be an opportunity to get to know the locals.' He tried to sound mildly enthusiastic, when really, meeting the locals was the last thing on his mind.

They had an early night. Sally was still tired, and she'd said nothing about the amazing sex session they'd just had. He'd half expected her to be a little coy, but she was just his normal Sal, albeit a very sleepy version. Almost as if it had never happened.

He was in the bathroom, when he heard her cry of dismay.

'Oh no!'

'What's up?'

She was crouched by the bed, looking at something on the floor. 'Oh! Poor little thing.'

'What is it?'

'A mouse.' She showed him the small brown body, stiff in her hands. 'It's dead, poor thing.'

Paul looked at Bluebell curled up on a chair. 'Bluebell, was this you?'

The cat gave him one of her disdainful looks and ran down the stairs.

'There'd be nothing left if she'd got hold of it,' said Sally. 'It must just have found its way in, and then died. I wonder why it died.'

'Animals do die, Sal. Give it here, I'll get rid of it.' He placed it in a bundle of tissues and took it downstairs. 'Wash your hands well, just in case.'

After disposing of the mouse in the outdoor bin, he went to go back inside when a sound stopped him in his tracks. It was like a baby crying – a haunting sound. For a second the sound disturbed him. Then realisation dawned, it was just Bluebell yowling.

'Bloody cat,' he murmured, going back inside. He shut the door, turning the key and shooting the bolt across. Tomorrow, he'd see about rigging up some security lights. This place was just too vulnerable. It was a bad idea not having lights, anybody could come creeping right up to the house. He was amazed that Sally felt so secure here. Didn't the girl ever get nervous?

He reached across the sink to close the kitchen curtains, aware that anyone could see right into the house, especially with the lights turned on. He was about to pull them together when something slammed into the window pane. 'Jesus!'

Instantly he switched off the kitchen light so the garden was illuminated by the moonlight and he could see out rather than anyone seeing in.

His heart dropped when he spotted the tawny feathers sticking to the outside of the glass. 'Ah no. Not the owl.'

He was out in a flash. As he'd thought, the owl was lying on the patio, flapping pathetically, struggling to right itself. His heart went out to it.

'Hey, you aren't meant to fly in to windows.' He spoke softly as he bent down beside it. 'I thought you owls were supposed to be wise.'

It continued its frantic flapping and Paul wondered whether he should cocoon it in a towel, or if that would stress it out even more and it would die of shock. But if he left it, it would be fox supper in no time – or Bluebell's.

'Sally!' he yelled back through the open door. 'Sally, come down, can you?'

A few moments later she appeared in slippered feet, her dressing gown hugged tightly to her chest. 'What's happen–' she saw instantly and gasped. 'Oh, the poor thing.'

'It flew into the window.'

'Do you think it's broken any bones?'

'I've no idea.'

'Well, we can't just leave it, hang on …' She raced indoors and returned with a tablecloth; she crouched close to the bird, speaking softly. She folded the linen around it and swaddled it like a baby.

Paul watched, quite in awe as her gentle movements seemed to calm the bird's terror a little. She got to her feel, cradling it in her arms, whispering soothing words. It stopped struggling.

'If it hasn't broken any bones, it might survive the shock. We could put it in your workshop, it'll be safe from predators.'

'Good idea,' Paul agreed, nipping inside for a torch. There were feathers on the kitchen floor, blown in by the wind. Outside, Sally was still cradling and crooning to the bird, her face quite close to its dangerous-looking beak. 'Careful, Sal. It could have your eye out.'

She glanced up and smiled. 'I think it likes me. Its heartbeat was frantic but it's slowing down now. It's stopped struggling, too.'

'Sal, don't build your hopes up too much. It's probably not going to survive.'

She glared at him. 'No. Don't say that. Besides its eyes are bright and it's moving its head like it's curious. Come on let's get it safely in your workshop.'

They settled the owl in a cardboard box on his workbench. Paul couldn't help wondering if they would find it dead in the morning.

He couldn't sleep. Long after Sally's soft rhythmic breathing had settled into a deep silence, he lay staring through the window at a star-studded sky. He wasn't quite sure what was disturbing him the most, that clumsy owl or memories of Petronella Kytella in the nursing home. He'd hardly thought about her all week but now she was back in his head. He wished to God he hadn't glanced back and seen her staring after him. If only he'd left thinking that she was in a world of her own. But her eyes had been sharp as pinpoints – and full of hate.

It wasn't just her face, either. It was the smell, and the feeling of panic as he'd tried to get away. Making his way across the care home lounge to the locked door, he'd been positive that she was on his tail, ready to smash him over the head with something.

A glimpse of memory or imagination – he didn't know which – flashed through his mind. A face looming above him, gnarled hands clutching a rock, coming at him. Then pain. A shooting pain through his skull, like he'd experienced on the day he'd arrived here.

Sally murmured and rolled over. It was just a memory of the pain, not real, he told himself ... just a memory. But his thoughts were drifting. Had the old woman really smashed his skull in that day when he was nine and he'd just burned her cat? Had she? Owen had said she'd appeared from nowhere and chased after them. They'd split up and the old woman had gone after him.

His breathing slowed as his thoughts drifted, and then something shifted in the shadows over by the wardrobe. There was something there. A feeling of dread crept over him. He dived out of bed, finding the light switch. He clicked it down, but nothing happened. The bedroom remained pitch black. Then a face, pale and ugly, sprang up right before his eyes. His yell of fright brought him wide awake and sitting bolt upright in bed.

A dream. Nothing but a damn nightmare, but he was sweating.

Sally slept on, barely stirring. He swung his legs out of bed and sat, head in hands. It had been years since he'd had a nightmare. Years since anything had scared him. What the hell was going on? He got up, badly needing a coffee.

Downstairs, he took a mug of black coffee through to the workroom and checked his emails. It was just after two and while he was alert enough to do some work, he certainly wasn't in the mood for it. His mind was elsewhere.

Maybe he should go back to the nursing home. Ask Petronella Kytella if she had smashed in the skull of a nine-year-old little boy forty years ago. No *maybe* about it. He'd *definitely* go back. His feelings of disdain for this woman were growing. She was playing on his mind far too much for his liking. He'd whisper in her ear that she couldn't play dumb with him. He'd tell her in no uncertain terms that he knew she'd tried to kill him when he was a nine-year-old kid. Yes, at the first opportunity he'd do just that.

Eventually he went back to bed. Sally slept on, oblivious. He was glad of that. No point in them both being baggy-eyed in the morning.

Concentrating on his decision to return to the nursing home when work allowed, Paul eventually slept. At some point in the night he felt something soft brush his cheek. In his dreams it was just Bluebell but then he felt the bed dip. He opened his eyes to see Sally getting up.

'You okay, Sal?' he asked drowsily.

She didn't answer, but walked out of the bedroom door. He listened for her going into the bathroom, but instead her soft bare feet descended the stairs in the dark.

He got up, almost tripping over the damn cat. 'Move Bluebell!'

Fully awake now, he followed her down and through to the kitchen, switching the lights on as he went. She stood at the back door in just her flimsy nightdress, and drew back the bolt. 'Sal … Sally, what are you doing?'

Still no answer. He stepped closer and turned her to face him. She stared straight through him, her eyes wide, pupils dilated, her face blank. Sleep-walking.

Instantly, Paul drew the bolt back across and gently took her hands, finding she was clutching her car keys. God. She wasn't intending to drive, was she?

'Back to bed, Sally,' he said softly, trying to stay calm, wondering what the hell had brought this on. In all the months of being together she had never sleep walked. Maybe it was the upset of the owl. Her next word confirmed his assumption.

'Sanctuary …' she murmured, allowing herself to be led.

'Yes, sanctuary, a nice soft, warm bed. Up the stairs now.'

Halfway up, Bluebell wrapped its body around Sal's legs.

'Bluebell! For God's sake will you stop trying to trip us up.'

It trotted downstairs and out of the cat flap. Once in the bedroom, Sally stood at the side of her bed, a vacant expression on her face. Paul gently pressed her shoulders so that she sat, then lifted her feet until she was lying down. He tucked the covers under her chin. Lying beside her, he watched her sleeping until the morning light crept in. Finally, he slept.

Sally woke him with a kiss. She'd brought tea and toast on a tray and balanced it expertly as she climbed back into bed with him. 'Morning, sleepy head. Cuppa?'
Paul eased himself upright, the events of the night unfolding as he sipped the hot brew. 'I need this.'

'I wonder how the owl is this morning,' Sally said as she drank her tea. 'I didn't want to check without you.'

He nodded. 'Sal, do you remember getting out of bed last night?'

'Nope, I don't think so.'

'Well, then you were definitely sleep-walking.'

She almost choked. 'Never!'

'I'm telling you, Sal, you were sleep-walking.'

'I was probably going to the loo.'

'You went downstairs and were trying to get out the back door.'
She stared at him. 'You are joking.'

He took a deep breath. 'And you had your car keys in your hand.'
'Oh my God!'

Paul put his cup down. 'You don't remember?'

She shook her head, stunned. 'No. I slept like a log last night, or I thought I did. I did have this dream of the owl though. I was so worried it might die. Then someone told me to take it to the animal sanctuary ...'

'You said *sanctuary*! The one and only word you said was sanctuary. I guess that's why you were sleep-walking.'
Sally stared wide-eyed at him. 'I was. In my dream there was someone telling me that's what I had to do.' She clutched his hand. 'I had to drive there ... Paul, I would have driven in my sleep!'

'No, you wouldn't have got that far,' he assured her, although deep down she had just voiced his worst fears. 'You'd have woken as soon as the cold air hit you.'

'Do you think so?'

'Without a doubt,' he promised, giving her a hug but thinking that tonight he would hide her car keys.

She looked thoroughly miserable. 'I've never sleep-walked before. Or at least, I don't think I have.'

'It was the upset of the owl,' Paul said, eager to check on the bird. Kissing Sally's cheek he got up. 'If it is alive and kicking, it might be an idea to get it checked out at that sanctuary.'

Sally said nothing, and when he raised one eyebrow at her, she murmured. 'I think I was a bit befuddled. There isn't a wildlife sanctuary around here. Not as far as I know, anyway.'

'Oh!' He felt quite sorry for her. She looked so confused. 'Come on. Let's go take a look at that mad bird.'

Paul threw on some working clothes and went downstairs, opening the living room curtains to a dull, misty-grey, Sunday morning.

The grass was soaked with dew and a chill mist hung over the garden. Sally slid her arm through his and they walked purposefully down to the barn.

Exchanging glances as he opened the door, he hoped the owl would come swooping over their heads to freedom. What he feared was that it would be stiff on its back with its legs in the air. What he saw, however, brought a smile to his face.

It was perched on top of a wooden roof beam, slightly ruffled but alert, with an indignant look on its face.

Sally gave a little squeal of delight and hugged him.

'The tough old bird.' Paul said, delighted.

'It's okay, isn't it?'

'Certainly looks it. And it's obviously flown up there, so no major damage done.'

She squeezed him, happily. 'What should we do?'

'Just leave it, I guess. We'll leave the barn door open, and it can fly out when it's ready. Or it can stay. I don't mind.'

Later they popped into the DIY store to buy outdoor lights and spotted Father Willoughby wandering around the aisles, his mind was clearly on his shopping as he paced past them, heading down the pest control aisle.

'He's miles away,' Paul murmured, macabrely remembering the myth about all the parishioners being poisoned. He was about to make a joke of it when Sally spoke.

'Probably thinking about his sermon for the funeral on Monday. What on earth can he say that's going to comfort anyone?'

'We don't have to go, you know, Sal.'

'I want to!' She sounded offended, then ashamed, as if she'd just remembered that it wasn't that many years since he buried his first wife. 'Sorry, I was forgetting. I don't mind going on my own, if …'

'I'm coming with you, Sal. I was just thinking about you.'

'What about me?'

He thought it best not to suggest she was maybe getting a bit stressed, hence the sleep walking. 'I don't want you upset, that's all.'

'It's Doctor Scott and his children who are upset, poor lambs.'

Finding the area selling security lamps, he was glad to change the subject as they discussed what was needed.

That afternoon he got the lights all wired up. As he worked he thought more about visiting the nursing home again to confront the old crone. For all he knew she could have attacked other kids. He'd look deeper into this once the Peace Conference was over and done with. It was just a month away. Get that out of the way first.

They'd left the barn door open all day and kept an eye on the owl. It looked perfectly at home perched on the beam, and just as it was growing dark and Paul was thinking what a nice companion it would be, it swooped out through the door and vanished into the woods.

He would liked to have spent a few hours on his carvings, but it seemed wrong to desert Sally on a Sunday evening. Reluctantly, he closed up the barn and walked up the garden, pleased by the way the halogen lights clicked on, triggered by his movement. The fact that it plunged everything else into pitch blackness was a by-product he would have to live with.

# Chapter 16

The weather suited the mood. The heavens opened and a biting cold rain lashed down as mourners gathered together. Paul stood arm in arm with Sally on the street outside Saint Mary Magdalene's church, huddled under an umbrella. It was a fine-looking church, typically Norman, with a tall clock tower and crenelated parapets. It seemed like the entire village had turned out to pay their respects to the doctor's wife.

The fact that Paul didn't know her was irrelevant. He remembered her widower, Adrian Scott. They'd gone to the same primary school. He remembered that the second he saw the bereaved man step out from the black limousine.

As a kid, Adrian Scott was always red nosed, always had a cold or an allergy or something. Bizarre, considering his dad was a doctor. Looking at him now, Paul couldn't tell if the red nose today was purely down to his grief.

Two weeping teenagers – a boy and a girl – clung onto their father's arms. Paul's heart went out to them, knowing the years of heartache and misery that stretched ahead. 'Poor souls.'

Sally squeezed his hand, as if feeling his pain. He folded the umbrella and joined the sombre congregation as they filed into the church.

The music was ridiculously cheerful – probably a favourite song of the deceased. She could never have guessed it would be her funeral anthem.

'There's Juliet and Owen,' Sally whispered, before they silently walked down an aisle and slid into the pew next to them. Owen turned and nodded his head in acknowledgement. His skin was unusually pale. Juliet was even greyer.

The coffin was set in the centre aisle, light oak with a beautiful grain. A framed photograph of an attractive smiling woman stood on the lid beside a tumbling arrangement of lilies and ivy. When the church seemed as full as it could be, the doors closed with a resounding clang. Candle flames fluttered, and the smell of incense and lilies filled the air. Paul tried not to think of Helena, but it was impossible.

The diminutive Father Willoughby made the Sign of the Cross, his voice more subdued than Paul had ever heard as he began the prayers for the Requiem Mass.

Between the silences, the sound of sobbing was continuous and wretched, and in the Homily the priest talked about the tragedy of the lovely, lively young wife and mother who had died so suddenly and tragically. There seemed no rhyme nor reason for her passing, and he reiterated the fact that God works in mysterious ways.

Why was it always God who got the blame? Why not the devil? Paul thought.

When it was time for the Eucharist, Sally and Juliet both went up to the altar. Heads bowed, they filed around the coffin set on its pedestal. Others joined the queue to receive Holy Communion or a blessing, leaving sparse people dotted about on the pews – the unbelievers or the sinners, Paul assumed. He was surprised to see Juliet in line to receive the priest's blessing, seeing as she was a white witch.

He leant towards Owen. 'A Christian witch, that's unusual.'

Owen slid along the pew, closing the space left by the two women. He whispered in Paul's ear. 'I'm in deep shit.'

Paul glanced at him. Whatever was troubling him, it was taking its toll. Owen was uncannily pale. 'What's wrong?'

'Been caught playing away, mate.'

Paul's initial reaction was to think his old pal was a stupid idiot. Couldn't he see what he risked losing? Keeping the irritation from his voice, and hoping Owen wasn't chasing sympathy, he murmured, 'Sorry to hear that. I thought you pair were pretty sound.'

'It was a one-off. Bloody stupid, I know. I just kind of got carried away and it happened.'

Paul stared at him. 'How did Juliet find out?'

His pale face hardened and his voice came out as a hiss. 'The bitch told her.'

'Jesus!' Paul gasped, causing the woman in front to turn with a glare of disapproval. He lowered his voice, noticing that Sally was just about to receive the Communion host. Irrationally, his thoughts strayed from his old mate's predicament to that story – the myth or whatever it was - of the congregation being poisoned. For a moment the thought was so strong that he almost shouted *Don't take the host!* But the story was seventy years old and probably not a scrap of truth in it, anyway.

Sally headed back, followed by Juliet, their heads bowed.

Under his breath Paul asked, 'Anyone I know?'

'You remember the witch's house?' said Owen.

How could he forget? He nodded.

'Well there's a different kind of witch living there now ...' he broke off, as Sally and Juliet slid into the pew.

Paul's jaw dropped. The blonde with the green eyes. The one he'd fantasised about not so long ago. The woman who'd hinted that he'd be welcome back at her door any time.

My God! If he'd done anything – not that he would have, not in reality, but if he had, then she might have come knocking on Sally's door. And their life together – his second chance at happiness – would have been over in a flash.

The fragility of it all made his head reel. It could all have been swept away so easily. One mistake. One wrong move.

The service continued but Paul found it hard to think about anything except those bewitching green eyes that could have been his downfall. At the end of the service Father Willoughby led the procession as they carried the coffin from the church.

The deceased's son's legs buckled and there was quite a commotion as he collapsed, distraught. The priest and coffin bearers moved on, but the congregation waited until the boy was back on his feet and was led, weeping inconsolably on his father's shoulder, out into the rain.

Juliet, with tears streaming down her face, linked Sally's arm and the two women walked on beneath an umbrella. Paul had no doubt that they were talking about Owen's misdemeanour. Owen shuffled along beside him, the arrogant swagger gone, head down and dejected.

'What am I going to do, Paul? Juliet means the world to me?'

'So why did you do it? I don't mean to get on my high horse, but if you're going to put it about, don't do it on your own doorstep.'

'I don't. It was a one off. Honestly. I'm telling you the truth.'

'So, you weren't seeing this woman regularly?'

'No. I can only put it down to thinking about how we used to knock the door and run like hell. It kind of tormented me, so I did it. I knocked the door. Just to see what would happen.'

Paul held his breath. He knew the next bit. 'And it was opened by a buxom, green eyed blonde who invited you in?'

Owen stared wide eyed at him. 'You've been there, too?'

'I knocked the door but that's as far as it went.' It wasn't the exact truth, but a fantasy doesn't count.

Owen pulled up his coat collar, rain streaming down his white face. Paul put his umbrella up, sheltering them both as the rain pelted down and the cold seeped through to the skin.

Ahead, the crowd had gathered around an open grave, and the coffin was lowered into the hole. The sound of sobbing was heartbreaking. Moving closer to the girls, Juliet flashed Owen a look of utter misery and turned away from him. Paul caught Sally's eye and her expression was one of uncertainty – what was to be done in this awful situation?

Father Willoughby began the graveside service as the wind blew and flapped his vestments and rain streamed down his face like the teardrops of the broken hearted.

'What do I do, Paul?' Owen pleaded. 'How the hell do I turn back the clock?'

'You can't, my friend. You'll just have to tell her you're sorry and keep telling her until she believes you,' Paul whispered, his eyes drawn then to a solitary magpie perched on a low branch of a tree.

*One for sorrow …*

It couldn't be more apt.

Earth to earth, ashes to ashes. They committed the body of Adrian Scott's wife to the ground, and one by one the people dispersed. Family back to the Scott's household, the rest to the Crow and Feathers. Paul needed to get home. He had work to do, and a carving to be looked at.

He was just about to suggest they head off when Juliet let out an almighty wail and shot across the street. Shrieking and cursing she lay into some woman walking by, pulling at her blonde hair and slapping her around the head. Paul recognised the green-eyed blonde immediately.

'Oh God!' Owen moaned, burying his head in his hands.

'Juliet, don't,' Paul yelled, sprinting across the road and hauling Juliet away from the startled blonde.

The woman looked terrified. 'Keep her away from me, please …'

'You whore! Bitch!' Juliet screamed, twisting in Paul's arms, desperately trying to get her hands on the woman again.

Sally ran across too, trying to calm her, but Juliet's eyes were wild. Paul hollered for Owen. He finally came over, his face bright pink now, as people stopped and stared.

The blonde backed away, looking outraged now rather than afraid. 'She needs locking up. The woman's insane.'

'You're the sort that needs locking up, you whore!' Juliet screamed.

'I don't know what the hell you're talking about,' the blonde snapped back.

Sally sprang to her friend's defence. 'You slept with her boyfriend. How do you expect her to react?'

Those green eyes blinked in total disbelief. It was a look that Paul felt wasn't faked. And when she protested, he had the strongest feeling that she meant every word.

'I haven't slept with your boyfriend! I don't even know your bloody boyfriend!'

Juliet wailed miserably. 'How dare you deny it? You came into my shop two days ago and told me how he fucked you!' Writhing in Paul's arms so she could turn back to Owen she screeched, 'See how much you mean to her? See!'

Owen slumped back against a wall, head in hands.

The woman turned on Juliet furiously. 'I haven't a clue what you're talking about. I haven't touched him and if I had, I certainly wouldn't have told anyone. Are you insane? Or do you think I am?'

She sounded convincing. 'Juliet, are you sure you haven't got the wrong woman?' Paul asked, not risking letting her go. Yet it was the blonde all right, the woman who had all but invited him in. She played a pretty cool game.

'Have I, Owen?' Juliet demanded, turning to him again. 'The least you can do is tell me the truth now. Is this her?'

Owen nodded miserably.

The blonde gasped. 'Oh, this is insane. You're as mad as each other!' She stormed away, glancing nervously back as if afraid of being followed by this crazy bunch of accusers.

The crowd dispersed, most ending up at the Crow and Feathers. Sally took over the job of holding onto Juliet, but now all she could do was weep on Sally's shoulder.

'Take her home, Owen,' Paul suggested. 'You can't undo what's been done. You're just going to have to prove how sorry you are, and how much you love her. If it's your first mistake, you might be lucky. She might forgive you.'

Owen stood awkwardly on the pavement, looking like he desperately wanted to hold his woman, but afraid of her reaction should he try.

Sally moved her friend gently, easing her into Owen's arms. Juliet flinched when he touched her, but she seemed drained and as his arm went around her shoulder she allowed him to lead her away.

Sally linked Paul's arm. 'What was all that about? Do you think she accused the wrong woman?'

'I don't think so, Sal. But she put on a damn good act of being innocent, didn't she?'

'That's what I thought, but I guess she doesn't want the whole village knowing what she's been up to. Anyway, Owen would have said if it was the wrong woman, surely. What a swine! Why are men never satisfied with what they've got?'

'Hey, I am,' he objected, hoping to God his guilt wasn't showing. Although he wasn't actually guilty of anything. It had been a fantasy, nothing more – and it never would be. Not if he had anything to do with it.

# Chapter 17

With the Peace Conference scheduled for three weeks' time, Paul spent the majority of the week at his London office working out a precise schedule to cope with fifty world leaders and Heads of State. Tensions were rising and he, along with Daniel Rake and some other key players, were invited to No. 10 to talk through security arrangements with the PM.

Paul never felt more at home and in complete control than when his human logistics were running like clockwork – even with his security now covering this small gathering. The pressure was always on his shoulders, but it was pressure that excited him. And it was good to see the PM again. They got on well, seeing eye to eye on many things. And she always seemed appreciative of his department's work. She was a charming woman despite being a cat lover. Her grey Persian barely left her lap throughout the meeting.

The Peace Conference would last three days: Wednesday the seventh until Friday the ninth, with the PM welcoming all the heads of state, prime ministers and top dogs from around Europe and the rest of the world. The safety of them, their security officials and entire entourage was down to Paul and his team. It was certainly going to be full on.

Later, in the car heading back to the office, Daniel Rake turned the conversation around to more personal affairs. 'So how are you settling into your new place, Paul? Does the rural life work for you?'

'It certainly does,' Paul agreed. 'Wildlife, fresh air, and I've even taken up something I used to do years ago.'

'Really? What's that then?'

There was a sudden unexpected eagerness to talk about his hobby. 'When I was a kid, I used to whittle away with a penknife and a bit of wood. I've kind of got back into that. But in a big way. Have a look at this.' He took out his mobile and brought up a photo of the bust. 'Who do you think this looks like?'

Rake's eyes widened. 'President Howard! It's damn good. What's your plans for it? Thinking of selling it?'

'Giving it away, actually,' said Paul. 'I've got an idea I'd like to run past you.'

'Go on.'

'Do you think the President might like it as a gift from the UK?'

'I should think he'd love it!'

Paul smiled. 'That exactly what Sally said.'

'So, what made you do a bust of him?'

Paul drew up his shoulders. 'It wasn't planned. I'd no idea what it would turn into when I started it. It was like being on auto pilot.'

'Well, it's first class, Paul,' said Rake. 'Pity you didn't mention it earlier, we could have got her ladyship's approval while we were at No. 10. Leave it with me and I'll get back to you about it.'

Paul rang Sally once they were back at Thames House. She was a while in answering, and in those few moments Paul felt a twinge of unease. He hoped to God she hadn't sleep walked again. And then the phone was answered, and Sally's cheerful voice greeted him. He breathed a sigh of relief. All was well.

It was Friday afternoon when he finally got a chance to return to his workshop. The carving of the reclining woman rested on his workbench covered by a piece of cloth. He hesitated, resisting the urge to unveil it and continue cutting away the excess wood to reveal the beauty within. The very fact that the pull and desire to do so was so intense made him stop … made him resist.

Instead he got a broom and swept up all the wood shavings. He went back to the house, made coffee and took a cup through to Sally as she machined her latest creation. He checked and dealt with his emails, but the pull was there, like a fishing rod reeling him in. Eventually, walking down the leaf strewn lawn to his workshop it almost felt like he was heading to an illicit rendezvous.

There was no need for the heater to be on. Despite the cold October day, he was on fire – his body burned as he handled the figurine. His chisel slid over her body, peeling her out of her wooden cocoon so that her naked form was revealed. It was no real surprise that it was her – the green-eyed vixen from the old woman's house.

Taking a strip of sandpaper, Paul worked on her delicate features and as she slowly revealed herself, so the desire to deliver the carving as a gift became almost overwhelming.

It was impossible not to make love to Sally when he finally closed the barn door for the night. The urge couldn't be ignored. But he was glad it was his lovely sweet Sally that he caressed and loved, and no fantasy running crazily through his head.

She cooked him dinner afterwards and sat in front of a blazing fire with Bluebell stretched across the back of an armchair. Helena wasn't in the flames any more. There had been only that one time, weeks ago now. She was at rest again.

'Have you heard how Owen and Juliet are getting on?' Paul asked as he gazed into a glass of ruby wine. 'Have they kissed and made up yet?'

Sally wrinkled her nose. 'I popped in to see her on Tuesday when you were in London and she was still furious at how that woman denied everything. I mean why be so brazen and tell the wife you've been sleeping with her partner one minute, then deny it the next? What's the point? I don't get it.'

'She's just a troublemaker, I guess. Some women are like that when they can't get what they want.'

'Are they?' Sally murmured. 'Well she's picked on the wrong woman there.'

'Why?'

'Well, Juliet is a witch, isn't she?'

'Meaning?'

'I told you, she's a white witch, only she's having some very black thoughts at the moment.'

Why was it that the mention of any kind of witch caused the hairs on the back of his neck to prickle? He tried to shrug it off, make light of it. 'Don't tell me she's mixing up a potion to get back at her.'

'That's exactly what she is doing!' Sally exclaimed, tucking her legs beneath her. 'After their skirmish, she ended up with a handful of her hair, and it's kind of given her the basis for a spell.' Her voice trailed away. 'It's not good, is it?'

'No, it's not! We need to talk to her.'

'She's too hurt, right now. It's just her way of getting it out of her system.'

Although it wasn't his place to tell a grown woman what she should or shouldn't do, he liked Juliet. He didn't want to see her make matters worse.

The following morning, Sally was snowed under with work. Paul decided to see Juliet alone. 'I'll take a couple of carvings along too, see if she wants them for her shop.'

'Which ones?' Sal asked, barely glancing up from her sewing machine.

'That ugly face one, though God knows who'd want it, and the nude.' He needed that gone. The desire was still there, nagging at him to call by the blonde's cottage and show her. And that would be suicidal.

'Oh, I'd love us to keep that one, it's beautiful. Get rid of the ugly one, though.' Sally stopped her sewing and looked at him. 'And Paul, be tactful. Juliet is struggling at the moment.'

He agreed, wishing he hadn't mentioned the nude.

Sally smiled. 'Thank you. You're an angel.'

He didn't feel much like an angel as he headed down to his workshop. Leaving the nude lying under her cloth, he took the *face* carving. It was bloody ugly. The face was thin and deeply lined. The texture of the skin – if you could call wood-bark skin, was rough, as if it had warts and lumps. He turned it this way and that, trying to find something pleasing to the eye, and failing. But then the eyes suddenly caught his. Deeply set and wrinkled, but the pupils were sharp as needles – and looking right into his.

'Jesus!' he yelped, instantly dropping the carving.

It was her. The old woman. Skin prickling, he backed away. But it remained looking right at him with eyes full of disdain.

Dear God, how could his subconscious have played such a trick on him?

Stumbling, he ran for the axe on the far wall, knowing what he had to do. He took it down and carried it back, his heart pounding so hard it was as if he was intending a real murder rather than the destruction of a bit of wood.

It was staring at him, its mouth set in a sneer that he hadn't carved. This was insane. It was just a block of wood. He needed to take this outside and destroy it. But as if it sensed his intentions, its eyes seemed to narrow, looking even more menacing.

The thought of touching it made his skin crawl. This couldn't be real. It was another nightmare. Even so, he grabbed one corner and threw it outside. At that split second, a stab of pain shot through his hand and he saw the splinter of wood sticking out of his palm like one of Christ's crucifixion nails. Blood trickled down his wrist.

There shouldn't be any splinters, those days were long gone. Yet the slither of wood he eased out of his hand was inches long.

After grabbing the rag off the reclining nude, he stemmed the blood. Then picking up the axe he went outside to finish the job.

At first, he couldn't see where it had landed and scoured amongst the shrubs before he saw it lying there. Harsh eyes glaring up at him.

'Right, you bastard!' He raised the axe above his head and brought it swiftly down, cleaving it in half. He stared into its ugly face, no longer intimidated. The life gone from it eyes.

But then it moved. Small jerky movements making it writhe. He backed off, transfixed. 'What the fuck ...'

As he stared, a darker shape separated from it. His hands tightened around the axe handle. But then came a small pointed head, and tiny feet. And when a hedgehog crept out from beneath the broken carving, laughter exploded like a released pressure valve.

He watched the little creature vanish into the mist. 'Run you little bugger, scaring me like that. You're lucky I didn't chop you in two …'

Using the axe head, he flipped one half of the carving on top of the other, took aim and sliced it into quarters. Finding a spade, he scraped up the remnants and dumped them onto the bonfire pile to burn when they next lit one up.

He placed the axe back in the barn, confusion settling over him. He could handle most things in life – gunfire, bombs, aggressive people – but this was something else. Was it him? Some glitch that the doctors hadn't fixed from the coma? He thought back to the embers in the fire and Helena's face, and the smell of burning hair and the irrational fears and nightmares … and now this.

'What the hell's happening to me?' he said quietly to himself.

'Paul!' Sally shouted from the kitchen door. 'Telephone!'

He was actually glad to be disturbed, though he wondered who'd ring him on Sal's house phone. His feet slithered on the wet grass as he headed towards her, his expression calm, determined she wouldn't see his agitation. There was no point in worrying her.

'What have you done to your hand?' she asked, linking his arm.

'Oh, nothing, just a slip with the chisel,' he lied. 'Who is it?'

'It's that care home. We left our number, remember? Seeing as we were the only people to have asked about that old lady. What was her name?'

'Petronella Kytella,' he said, knowing what was coming; she was dead. And he'd killed her. His throat felt like it had closed up. 'She's died?'

Sally cast him a curious glance. 'No! Just the opposite. The nurse says there's been a remarkable change in her, and they wanted us to know.'

Paul's eyes closed. He ought to be relieved that chopping up an effigy of the old dear hadn't actually finished her off. But knowing she was still alive – that those harsh, unforgiving eyes could still look at him – left him feeling totally unnerved.

He picked up the phone, positive it was going to be her cursing him to hell for putting an axe through her head.

The gentle familiar Irish lilt of the nurse made him sway.

'… we wanted you to know, seeing as you'd been good enough to come and visit her. Like I said, she doesn't get visitors, and we're so excited, we wanted to share it with someone, and you …'

'Yes, yes, her only visitors,' Paul repeated, quickly thinking up an excuse for not visiting her, which he knew would be coming next.

'Today would be a grand day to see her at her best,' the nurse went on. 'You might get some sense out of her.'

'It's not possible today,' Paul cut in abruptly. 'I've a train to catch to London, my job …' Sally shot him a puzzled look which he ignored. Wild horses wouldn't drag him back to that care home right now. He wanted to see her all right, but on his terms. He didn't like being manipulated, which was how this felt.

A calmness spread through him. Years of military training returned, helping him control his thoughts. 'So how is she, exactly?'

The nurse sounded glad to be asked and her intake of breath indicated she'd got a story to tell. Paul longed to hang up. 'Well, she was her usual self, semi-conscious, just about managing to wake up for a bit of food and drink when not ten minutes ago, she suddenly shot up out of her chair like the devil had pinched her backside. Cursing and swearing she was. It took two nurses to settle her down. That's amazing isn't it? We didn't even know she could stand up straight like that, and my, she's tall. When she's not all bent double, she's a mighty tall woman.'

Paul could feel bile burning in his throat. It wasn't possible. He struggled to find some rational explanation. 'Has she gone back to sleep now?'

'Not a bit of it,' laughed the nurse. 'She's sitting in her chair, grinding her teeth and banging her hands on the chair arms like she's itching for a fight. We can't get over it. Most of the staff have never seen her awake, let alone getting into a paddy.'

The room was beginning to spin. 'Maybe you should sedate her.'

'Oh, dear Lord, no. We're hoping that once she's had a nice cup of tea and a piece of cake, she'll feel like having a chat. We're all dying to hear about her life, where she's from and all that.'

'And you think she *will* settle down, not just get angrier and ...' his voice trailed away. What did he expect her to do? What was she capable of? He didn't know. Although actually, he did know one thing she was capable of – smashing a nine-year-old kid's head in with a rock.

Sally was staring at him, puzzled, wanting to know why he'd lied about having to go to London. 'What's happened?'

He told her. At least he told her what the care home had said. He kept silent about hacking her effigy to pieces.

'So why don't you want to see her now she's awake,' puzzled Sally.

He tried to shrug it off, as if it didn't matter. 'There's no point in raking up the past. She'll have forgotten the little brats who tormented her. Why drag up old memories?' Even to his own ears it sounded totally at odds to what he'd said before.

Sally looked long and hard into his eyes, trying to read the bits he'd missed out. 'Well, it's your decision, but will you forgive yourself if she dies before you get a chance to apologise?'

'I'll live with it,' he answered, thinking that Petronella Kytella also had a lot to be sorry for if his intuition and memories were anything to go by.

All too clearly now, in his mind's eye he could see a snarling ugly face bearing down on him as he'd fallen in the forest. She was clutching a rock. He remembered clearly as it slammed down on his head. Then pain, then blackness.

Sally's hands squeezed his. 'I wish you'd tell me.'

He suddenly needed to tell her. To share this horrible idea that had gotten into him. He took a deep breath. 'Sal, I could be mistaken, but I think it's possible that she's to blame for me being in that coma when I was a kid.'

'No!' she gasped. 'Why?'

He took a deep breath. 'Well according to Owen, she'd chased us ... that day in the woods. We'd been right little brats, so it seems, and I was the one she chased. It's assumed I fell and hit my head, but I've got this picture in my mind of her bashing me with a rock.'

'Oh my God.'

'I could be wrong. Imagination's a powerful thing.'

She looked incensed. 'What kind of a woman would do that to a child? She could have killed you – almost did kill you!'

Well, I'd killed her cat, he thought – just about stopping the words forming in his mouth and spitting them out. He couldn't believe he'd done that. But all too clearly, he could see a cat burning to death amongst the flames of a bonfire. He seriously wondered if Owen's version of what happened was the true story.

He kissed Sally softly on the lips. It was a thank-you-for-caring kind of kiss. 'We'll let it drop, Sal. I don't want to see her right now, that's all.'

'I should think not!' she said, outraged. 'I wouldn't mind going around there and questioning her about that day myself, even if she is old–'

'No! Don't go anywhere near that woman,' he stopped her. 'There's more to her than meets the eye.'

'What do you mean?'

'Bear with me on this, Sal. I know it sounds crazy, but with all these strange things happening lately, it's making me wonder. Is she just a confused, hate-filled old woman? Or could it be something darker? Could she actually be a witch? Which one?'

Without any carvings to take to Juliet's shop, Paul spent the remainder of the day at his computer. Sally didn't ask why he'd changed his plans, and he didn't bring the subject up. The more he thought about his actions earlier, the more ridiculous they seemed. He'd overreacted, allowing his mind to play tricks on him.

Determined to put the whole episode out of his head, he looked forward to Sally's suggestion that tomorrow they have Sunday lunch at the Crow and Feathers. For the first time since moving in with Sally and discovering his workshop, he didn't feel the urge to do any wood carving.

Later that afternoon the care home rang again. His heart sank as the now familiar Irish voice came on the phone.

'I thought I'd better tell you, just in case you happened to change your mind and visit after all. I didn't want you wasting your time …'

She's dead? Hope surged again.

'Only she's slipped back again. Lost with the fairies just like before, like always.'

Paul doubted she was with the fairies.

'There's something else,' the nurse said, just as Paul was about to thank her for the information and hang up.

He didn't want to know what the *something else* was, but he listened anyway.

There was a hint of reluctance in the Irish voice. 'Well, when she was awake and shouting blue murder, we noticed a nasty red line down her face. Like she'd fallen and hit herself. But she hasn't had a fall. There was a member of staff with her every second that she was up and on her feet.'

A parched feeling spread up his throat. He pictured himself slamming the axe through the wood carving's face. 'Was it a cut? Was she bleeding?'

'No, nothing like that. It was like she'd just walked into something with a sharp edge.'

Like an axe, he thought.

'Like a door,' said the woman. 'It must have been the arm of the chair, she'd been sat slumped.'

'I see.'

'I wouldn't like you to think we'd been negligent.'

'That's the last thing I'd think,' he heard himself say. So, she'd gone back to sleep. He'd rather she'd died in her sleep. 'It's good of you to keep us informed.'

'Well you're the only living connection we've got for her.'

'Yes, so it seems,' he agreed quietly. 'Let me know if there's any change.'

'I'll do that, indeed.'

He hung up, feeling sick, convinced now there was more to this woman than met the eye.

# Chapter 18

*A touch is all I need then they are mine. I make them dance like stringed puppets. Others see and fail to understand. What joy as I leave them with confusion and no memory of my presence.*

Sunday brought a sharp frost and Sally insisted on wrapping up in scarves and gloves and walking into the village through the woods. The trees were pretty stark now although the holly bushes were a dark glossy green waiting for berries to form. It made Paul think of Christmas and that brought a vague feeling of joy to his soul.

'So, what did your boss think of giving the bust of the President to him at the Conference?' Sally asked, as they made their way along the path.

Paul smiled. 'He had to check it with the PM, and I heard back that she thought it was a good idea. I'm not getting too excited though – President Howard probably won't want it.'

'He'll love it!'

'It probably won't even get past US security. They'll want it scanned and God knows what in case it's got a bomb inside.'

She cast her eyes heavenwards. 'People are so suspicious these days.'

'That's the kind of world we live in, sadly.'

She snuggled closer to him as they walked. 'And was your boss impressed with your carpentry skills?'

Paul loved her in this kind of mood. It had been a while since she'd been so carefree. 'He seemed to think it was a good likeness.'

'Good? It's fantastic!' Sally exclaimed. 'I'd just love for Juliet to see it, and get her reaction.'

He was still keen to see Juliet to sort out this revenge witch thing on the blonde. 'Okay, we'll see what she has to say, but let's keep our plans for it to ourselves.'

'Anyway, that other carving – the nude. I love that! It will look good on the mantlepiece.'

'It's okay,' he shrugged.

Sally laughed. 'Okay! My eye. It's brilliant and you know it. Oh! You haven't brought that plaque. We could have popped in and asked Juliet about it.'

That plaque was now in pieces on the bonfire heap. No need to tell Sally that, however. 'We don't need a reason to call on her, do we? How about we just knock the door and see if she and Owen – if he's around – want to join us for lunch?'

Sally beamed. 'Yes, that would be nice.'

'We'll do that, then,' said Paul, hoping also to gain some first-hand knowledge on the darker side of witches.

Juliet lived over her shop, and she was a long while in answering the doorbell. As they waited, Paul noticed some of his carved ornaments still in the shop window. It didn't surprise him. He didn't hold his work in high esteem. It really was just Sally looking at them through rose-tinted glasses.

He finally saw movement through the darkened shop interior and then Juliet opened the glass shop door. Chimes tinkled, and the scent of fragrant candles and incense wafted out. There were shadows under Juliet's eyes, but at least she hadn't got that downtrodden look about her. Just the opposite, in fact.

'Juliet! How are you?' Sally greeted her. 'We're just going to the Crow and Feathers for lunch. We wondered if you and Owen wanted to join us … if you're talking, that is.'

'Or even if you're not,' Paul added. 'We were actually hoping that we could match-make.'

Juliet gave a kind of snort, as if to say – yeah, like that's going to happen! Then she half smiled. 'Nice thought, but Owen's not here and I'm not hungry.' Seeming to remember her manners, she stepped back. 'Come in for a coffee, if you like.'

Sally glanced at Paul, gauging his reaction. He tried not to give away the fact that he was curious to ask her about witchcraft. He desperately wanted to know whether it was psychological and all in the mind, or whether it did actually hold some kind of power, a power that could change physical things in life? He took a step forward. 'You're sure we're not disturbing you?'

'Nothing that won't wait. Come on through.' Juliet locked the door after them.

There was a narrow stairway at the back of the shop that led up to her flat. Paul had to duck his head as he climbed the stairs. Looking around the small room, it appeared that she'd furnished her living room with left-over stock. It was colourful, mismatched, cluttered and fragrant. Somehow it seemed just right for a white witch.

'Coffee? Tea? I've all sorts,' said Juliet. 'I'm into honey and ginger at the moment.'

He and Sally squeezed together on the chintzy little sofa with its lacy arm covers. 'Black coffee, please, Juliet,' he said, moving a knitting bag to one side. It looked like she was halfway through creating a sweater. He vaguely hoped it was for Owen.

'My usual, white, no sugar,' Sally called, reaching across to examine the half knitted green garment. 'Wish I could knit. Actually, I've been thinking about mixing leather patches in with knitted squares for a shoulder bag. I think it would look quite good, kind of hippy.'

'There's a thought,' Paul agreed. 'You should suggest it. She could probably do with something to take her mind off *you know what*.'

'Maybe,' Sally murmured, placing the sweater back in the bag as her friend returned. Sympathetically she asked, 'How are things, Juliet? Have you got to the bottom of it, yet? Have you forgiven him?'

Juliet sank dejectedly into an armchair. She thought for a moment before answering. 'I can't forgive him, Sal. I've tried, really I have, because he's pretty cut up. Well he would be, wouldn't he? He's lost me, and that woman has disowned him, so he's lost out big time.'

Sally spoke softly. 'Hasn't he tried to explain? Were they having an affair, or was it just a one-off fling?'

Juliet ran her fingers through her hair. It was already wild. 'He says he doesn't know what came over him. A moment of insanity. And I'm supposed to accept that?'

*There but for the grace of God,* thought Paul. 'I'm sure he regrets it, Juliet. And is it really worth letting her win? Which she has, you know, if you allow this to break you up.'

Juliet went to say something then got to her feet. 'Kettle's boiled.'

Sally glanced sadly at him. Her expression seeming to say she doubted they were ready to kiss and make up just yet. They remained silent until Juliet came back with their drinks.

Juliet sipped her tea, holding a delicate bone china mug between two hands as if she needed its warmth to keep her functioning. 'I *want* to forgive him. But I just can't. It's like I've got this ball of anger lodged here in my chest which won't allow it. Maybe when I've got my rev ...' She stopped, looking slightly embarrassed and took another sip of tea.

'Got what?' Paul asked, knowing full well what she was about to say. When she'd got her revenge.

Juliet's voice rose angrily. 'Well for heaven's sake, she can't do this! She can't just seduce other women's partners and expect to get away with it. She needs to be taught a lesson.'

'And how are you going to do that?' Paul asked steadily, watching her face, seeing the slight trembling of her hands.

She turned aside. 'It doesn't matter how.'

'I think it does.'

Sally nudged him. 'Paul, if she doesn't want to explain, she doesn't need to.'

Turning away from Sally, he asked, 'What's it to be, a spell? Pins in a doll?'

Juliet glared at him as if he'd just hit the nail on the head and Paul struggled to quell the disconcerting feelings that he was talking to a witch – albeit a white one.

Quietly she said, 'An effigy is most effective.'

He kept his tone light. 'Okay then, is there any proof that doing what you're thinking of doing will make a difference or is it just to make you feel better in yourself?'

She gave a harsh little laugh. 'It's definitely going to make me feel better.' Then met his gaze. 'Don't underestimate these powers, Paul, I know you think it's all mumbo-jumbo. Many people have underestimated witchcraft, wicca, or whatever you want to call it – to their regret.'

'But you're a white witch!' Sally exclaimed, accusation in her voice. 'You're not supposed to dabble in the dark side of all this.'

Juliet lowered her eyes again. 'I know that and I'm not proud of it, Sally.'

'So, what are you thinking about doing?' Paul asked.

'It's probably best I don't tell you,' said Juliet.

But you're planning something,' Paul went on, needing to know. 'What do you do, concoct a spell?'

'Paul, witches long ago learned not to blab about what they do. They used to burn them at the stake, remember?' She took another sip from her cup. 'But what I will say is, all kinds of things can be achieved as long as you have something tangible in which to centre your spell, if you want to call it that. Something physical, with life in it. Not totally inanimate.'

'So, what you're telling me is that white witches can cast dark spells?' said Paul, seeing by her expression that he was right. 'Therefore, witches from the darker side of the occult would certainly be able to physically hurt other people and make their lives hell?'

Juliet looked steadily at him, then took a deep breath. 'Like all things in life, some people are stronger than others, some are cleverer than other, some people get angrier quicker than others, and some witches are far more powerful than others. It depends on who they're involved with. For example, are there any warlocks involved?'

'Warlocks?'

'Yes, or the devil!'

Sally almost choked on her coffee.

'You mean the actual devil?' Paul reiterated.

'Yes, the actual devil,' Juliet repeated, staring in exasperation at him. 'I don't think you really understand, Paul. Dark witches are satanic. There is no good side to them. And of course, it depends on their relationship with the devil. For example, if they have done something before that's pleased Satan, then they will be working with his power behind them.'

'Nice prospect,' Paul said quietly, her words confirming his worst fears. Not that he wanted to share that with either of them.

'It's a fact,' she shrugged.

He'd thought it before, and now he was even more convinced that this was something Juliet needed to steer well clear of. 'Juliet, I understand your anger, but revenge by witchcraft is not a good road for you to be going down.'

'Plus,' Sally added, 'You're a white witch, not a dark one.'

Paul leant towards her. 'Not to mention that cases of revenge resulting in any harm to another person are frowned upon by the law. You could lose your liberty, lose your business, your whole life could change for ever over this one incident.'

Juliet stared from one to the other, and then without another word she got up and went into another room. They waited silently.

Juliet returned, balancing something on the palm of her hand. Upon noticing what it was, Paul felt an icy prickle on the back of his neck.

It was a small rag doll, no more than three inches long, sewn from an old scrap of material, strands of blonde human hair sewn onto its head, and two long hat pins sticking through its chest.

Sally clasped her hands over her mouth. 'Juliet! No, that's so wrong. I can't believe you'd make something as vile as that.'

Juliet stared at it, almost laughing at her efforts. 'It's rubbish, isn't it? I'm sure I could have done better. But that is her hair.'

'And has it worked?' asked Paul calmly.

Juliet shrugged one shoulder, but then her face crumpled. 'I don't know.'

Paul had a sudden image in his head of slicing through the woodcarving with his axe. *We noticed a nasty red line down her face.* He looked steadily at Juliet and the effigy of the blonde. Then slowly and deliberately he stood and pulled the pins out of the doll.

A shrill buzz made all three of them jump.

Juliet's pale face twitched. 'Someone's at the door.'

'I'll go,' Paul said, not allowing his imagination to run away with him. He had no doubt, due to the expression on the two women's faces that a certain blonde might be standing, outraged, at the door. They followed him downstairs and through the shop.

The sight of Father Willoughby standing there took him totally by surprise.

Juliet seemed pleased to see him. 'Oh, I know what he wants.' She turned and ran back upstairs, shouting back over her shoulder, 'Open the door for me, would you, Sal.'

Father Willoughby looked vaguely surprised at seeing him and Sally standing there. 'Well, good day to you. Is the fine lady of the house at home?'

'She's just gone to fetch something,' said Paul, trying to gauge whether the priest was here on a mission to stop a black magic ritual, or calling round for a set of lace armchair covers.

'How are you, Father?' Sally asked, looking guilty as sin.

'I'm as the good Lord intended, very well, thank you. I didn't see you at Mass this morning, Paul.' His overly large eyes glinted behind his magnifying lenses. 'I imagine your work keeps you occupied? Are you involved at all with this Peace Conference we're hearing about in the news?'

'Only in a very small capacity, for my sins,' Paul agreed.

'We are all sinners,' stated the priest, 'and sin and evil are all around us. There are times when you can sense it in the air.' He fumbled for something in his overcoat pocket and brought out the small wooden cross that Paul had made for him. 'It's a coincidence that you're here because I'm picking up a chain for the cross you so kindly gave me.'

Paul felt quite humbled.

Juliet returned with a silver-coloured chain. 'Will this do, Father?'

'I couldn't have chosen better.'

She took the wooden cross and threaded the chain through the hole. 'There! It's not too girly and it won't break easily.'

'Superb,' he said, stroking the wood before tucking it under his woollen scarf. 'How much do I owe you?'

Juliet held up her hands. 'Nothing. My pleasure.'

*My penance is what you actually meant*, Paul thought to himself.

Sally hooked her arm through his. 'We ought to be going.'

'And I'll not hold you up any longer, either,' said the priest. 'I've a few home visits to make. Maybe I'll see you all next Sunday at Mass?'

'We'll try,' said Sally. 'Oh, Paul can't. He'll be in London, won't you?' She looked quite proud for a second but a glance from Paul stopped any boast of pride she was about to mention.

The priest nodded. 'Ah yes, all those world leaders, some no better than dictators and terrorists. It's an evil world we live in. The only answer is prayer.'

'Say a prayer for us then, Father,' said Paul.

'I'll offer Mass for your intentions,' replied the priest, looking up steadily into Paul's eyes. 'May God be with you.'

For a moment no one spoke and then Sally broke the silence. She turned and hugged Juliet. 'We'll be going. I'll pop in again during the week. I wanted to ask your opinion on something else Paul is working on.'

'I'll look forward to it,' said Juliet, turning to Paul. She kissed his cheek, whispering, 'Thank you for stopping me from making a massive mistake.'

He felt relieved, positive she wasn't going to be dabbling in any other black magic pranks.

The village street was fairly quiet, except for a woman walking a Staffordshire bull terrier on the other side of the road and one or two cars going by. One honked and Juliet and Father Willoughby both raised their hands in recognition.

'That's Mr and Mrs Clark,' said Juliet. 'Wave, Paul, she's one of your best customers.'

'Huh?'

'She's bought a few of your ornaments.'

'Really?' He turned, hand half raised, just as the dark blue Renault the couple were driving in slammed head-first into the side of a house.

The sound of crumpling metal and splintering glass seemed to go on and on. Bricks tumbled, crashed, bounced. The whole back end of the car lifted off the ground, as if it was trying to burrow deeper into the side of the house. A horn blared and then stopped.

Sally and Juliet screamed.

Father Willoughby stumbled backwards against the wall. 'Lord almighty!'

'Ring an ambulance,' Paul yelled, already halfway across the road, sprinting towards the chaos. His thoughts were racing, seeing which parts of the car were accessible. The car looked as if it was embedded midway inside the house, but as he got nearer, he saw it was just crushed, like you'd crush a tin can. He could see through the smashed driver's side window that the two occupants weren't screaming. They didn't even look like they were panicking. They both sat upright in their seats. Mrs Clark's left hand was slightly raised, as if she was still waving. Still waving at the nice man who carved those pretty ornaments and Father Willoughby who'd welcomed them to Mass that morning.

The air bags had inflated and burst. They were dark red in colour. Mrs Clark's must have burst when the gearbox had slammed through the chassis and landed in her lap, while Mr Clark's air bag had been punctured as the steering column ran through his chest.

He yelled at the woman with the dog heading towards them over of the revving engine. 'Keep back, there's nothing you can do.' Reaching through the window he turned off the ignition, then felt for a pulse on the man's neck.

A jolt, like a punch or an electric shock hit him, and the smell of burning hair filled his nostrils. He jumped back in time to see the dog straining on its leash, barking furiously as if protecting its owner from him. The lead suddenly shot out of her grasp and the dog flew at him, snapping at his ankle. Instantly the smell was gone, replaced by pain. With a yelp like someone had kicked it, the dog shot off towards the woods.

Father Willoughby gave the couple the Last Rites while the police cordoned off the area. The fire service began to cut through the wreckage to free what was left of Mr and Mrs Clark. Paul gave a statement to a police officer, showing him his ID. All thoughts of a nice lunch at the Crow and Feathers were gone, and eventually, they headed back through the woods towards home.

In his head he was trying to work out what had happened. Not only why a local would suddenly underestimate a familiar road and plough into the side of a house. But also, what happened when he touched the driver. The jolt had been like electricity, and why that smell for God's sake? He didn't wonder why the dog had bitten him, poor thing must have been frightened by the chaos.

He saw the tears in Sally's eyes. 'Are you okay?'

'Not really, Paul. Why didn't he see the bend in the road?'

'I'm asking myself the same question. Something could have gone wrong with his car, a puncture, steering failure, anything. He could have had a stroke, or maybe someone was sticking pins in a doll somewhere.'

She shot him a look. 'That's not funny.'

'You're damn right it's not.'

Following the leaf strewn pathway, they saw the woman and the staffie heading towards them.

'You found your dog, then,' Paul said.

'Yes, I'm ever so sorry that he bit you. He's not usually like that.'

Paul's thoughts flew back to when Bluebell had sunk her teeth into Sally's hand. The cat had acted out of character, too.

The woman continued. 'Something spooked him as you jumped back from the car. I thought you'd had an electric shock, are you all right?'

'I'm fine, don't let it worry you.'

'Did … did the people in the car survive?'

Paul shook his head. 'I'm sorry, I'm afraid not. It was very quick.'

She nodded, and tears welled up in her eyes. 'I thought not. You'd be best getting the doctor to look at the bite. I'm Doctor Scott's receptionist, I can get you straight in. Poor man, we buried his wife not five minutes ago and now another awful tragedy.'

'I know,' murmured Sally. 'It never rains but it pours.'

The woman gave a gentle tug on her dog's lead. 'Life goes on though – for some, anyway. Come on Buster. Let's get home.' She cast them a small smile. 'Take care.'

'Bye.' Sally replied for both of them. 'Bye, Buster.'

# Chapter 19

The memory of the dead woman's hand raised in a wave, locked in a split second of time, stayed in Paul's mind for days. It was bizarre how many strange and unexplained things were happening lately.

All this talk of witches and witchcraft needed looking into. Yet deep down, Paul felt it hard to actually believe there was any substance to it. The mark down Petronella's face and him chopping the carving in two could be pure coincidence. He was still pondering the situation when he took a break from his work in his office at the cottage to wander down to the barn.

He picked up the wood carving of the reclining figurine, his thoughts straying automatically to the blonde. Running his fingers over the delicate, perfect curves, he thought of Juliet pushing hat pins into an effigy of the woman. Had her spell worked? Had the blonde suffered, perhaps thinking she'd got acute appendicitis? Maybe gone to the doctor? Or was *she* lying dead in the cottage? Juliet's black magic spell going the whole hog and removing her from the scene totally?

Placing the figurine back on his bench, he closed the barn door and headed back to the house. Sally was machining a red lining fabric into a black leather shoulder bag. He stood behind her, his hands lightly manipulating her slender shoulders, still lost in thought.

'Not in the mood for woodwork?' she mused, turning her head slightly so that her cheek caressed the back of his hand.

'No, I'm not. And it just occurred to me that maybe Juliet's hocus pocus thing with the doll and pins might have worked.'

Sally paused in her sewing. 'Well she's stopped now. I think we made her see reason.'

'But what if it was too late?'

Sally swivelled in her chair to look up at him. 'What do you mean?'

'What if the damage has already been done?'

Her blue eyes winced. 'Hurt her, you mean?'

'Or worse. Has anyone see her about lately?'

She gasped. 'That's not possible! It's all rubbish, isn't it?'

All Paul could do was shrug again. 'I wish I could say for sure that it was. But I can't.'

Sally left the half-sewn bag on her workbench. 'What do we do?'

'We need to check on her.'

She got to her feet. 'What? Knock her door and ask if she's been suffering from shooting stomach pains recently?'

'Just check she's alive, I suppose.'

'Oh my God.'

There was a dire sense of urgency, suddenly. No thought this time of taking a leisurely walk to town through the woods. The need was to get there, and get there fast.

They parked in the street and Paul led the way down the little lane towards the old cottage, trying to think up some reason for knocking on her door. Maybe it would be better if Sally did the talking. Would the blonde remember Sal from the street fracas on the day of the funeral?

'What are we going to say?' Sally hissed as the grey-stone cottage came into view.

Even now, so many years since he was a kid, the sight of the witch's house brought his skin out in goose-bumps. There was a crow sitting on the chimney. There was always a crow. He tried not to look at it, but sensed it watching them.

'We'll just say we were concerned about her and wanted to check she was all right.'

'Say nothing about the doll, you mean?'

'Best not …' he stopped. She was just coming out of her front door as they approached her home, dressed in a red belted coat and knee length boots. She checked her door was locked, walked up the path, through the little gate when her eyes locked onto them.

For a second there was a flash of recognition, no doubt she remembered them as the friends of the mad woman who'd accused her of sleeping with her man.

Neither Paul nor Sally needed to say a word. The haughty look on her face and the speed in which she marched past them and up the lane proved that she wasn't suffering from any sharp, mysterious pains. And that was all that mattered.

He and Sally kept walking, as if they were taking a stroll in the woods. Only when they guessed she had reached the street did they stop and look back. Looking at each other's stiff faces, Sally suddenly creased up in giggles and flopped against Paul's chest, shaking with laughter.

It was infectious, and Paul found the whole thing just as hilarious. He gave in to the moment, glad to have something to laugh about for once. It had been quite a while.

'What shall we do now, then?' Sally finally asked, wiping a tear from her eye. 'Oh, we are a couple of idiots letting our imaginations run away with us. I know, let's pop in and see Juliet. See if there's any news about her and Owen making up.'

Paul slid his arm around her shoulders and turned her around to go back the way they'd come. 'May as well. We'll keep mum about this, though. If she knows she hasn't caused any suffering, she might give it another go.'

Walking back through town, they passed Father Willoughby's church. He was just outside the presbytery, taking something from the boot of his car.

Sally gave him a little wave, but for once the priest's mind was elsewhere and he looked right through them.

'Do you think he's okay?' Sally frowned.

'I doubt it. Losing three parishioners in such a short space of time can't have done him much good.'

'Poor man,' murmured Sally. 'I wonder how he's going to write this Sunday's sermon? God surely does work in mysterious ways.'

'So everyone keeps saying,' Paul remarked.

There was scaffolding up around the building that the car had smashed into, and workmen were repairing the damage. Paul glanced briefly then pushed open Juliet's shop door. The bell chimed its usual cheerful little tinkle as they went in. Fragrances of candles and oils wafted around them.

The shop was deserted, and Paul checked to see which of his carvings hadn't sold. The clogs and the walking stick were left. Maybe they'd be bought up as Christmas presents, not that it mattered to him one way or the other.

They browsed the shelves for a few moments, waiting for Juliet to appear. Eventually, Sally raised her eyebrows. 'Good job we're trustworthy, we could have made off with the takings and all her stuff by now.'

'Worth giving her a shout?'

Sally nodded and walked to the bottom of the stairs. 'Juliet. Hello. Anyone at home?'

There was no response and frowning, Sally started up the stairs. 'Think I'll just pop up. Hello Juliet, it's me … Sally, I'm coming up.' A moment later she screamed. A shriek of horror. 'Paul, call an ambulance!'

After jabbing the nine button three times as quickly as he could, Paul sprinted up the stairs, heart hammering. Dear God, now what?

The operator was asking which service he required.

'Ambulance!' he breathed, taking in the sight that met him.

Juliet was lying on the floor, unconscious in a pool of blood. Her knitting needles protruding from her chest and abdomen like a life-sized voodoo doll.

'Jesus.'

'Sir, are you there? Which service do you require?'

'Ambulance.' he spat out again, before providing the address. 'And the police … Sally, get towels, pad them around the wounds, try and stop the blood, don't take the needles out.'

On his knees, his trousers soaking up Juliet's blood, he checked for a pulse. There was a faint beat. He passed the details to the operator, doing what he could to stop the bleeding.

'Did she fall, do you think, Paul? Did she fall on her knitting? She looks …' Sally's face was white with shock.

He knew what she was thinking. She looked like the effigy Juliet had made. The knitting still on the needles had been green wool, now it was stained deep red.

'Ring Owen!' Paul barked. 'Have you got his number?'

'No, no, I haven't. You've got it, haven't you?

Downstairs the shop bell tinkled, and Owen called out to Juliet.

Sally gripped his arm. 'Oh my God, Paul!'

Paul hurried to stand in the doorway, arms held out, wanting to warn his old mate what he was walking into. But Owen was suddenly present in Juliet's little sitting room. His face lit up for a second on seeing his friends, and then he saw what was beyond Paul – the woman he loved sprawled on the blood-soaked rug. He wailed. A long, mournful, dreadful wail that was heartbreaking to the ear.

Owen fell on his knees, arms floundering, not knowing what to do to help. Tears streamed down his face, sobbing her name over and over.

'Put some pressure on the wounds, Owen,' Paul instructed. 'She's got a pulse, just try and stem the blood. Don't disturb the needles.' Then he spoke urgently into his mobile. 'That ambulance needs to be here, now!'

Later that evening, as the two of them sat quietly, Sally said softly, 'Paul, I meant to tell you something, but with all the commotion I didn't get chance.'

He touched her hand. 'Go on.'

'When I walked into Juliet's sitting room, I swear I saw a bird flying out of her window. Maybe it had startled her, and she fell.

Her stabbing herself like that doesn't necessarily mean it was her spell gone wrong, turned back on herself. Because that's what you're thinking, isn't it?'

'Something along those lines,' Paul agreed. 'What kind of bird was it?'

'It was big and black. I think it was a crow.'

He rubbed his temples, in an attempt to rid himself of the dull ache.

'Shit!'

# Chapter 20

*Use my magic and risk my future plans and I will turn it back on you. I shall stab your soul with my hatred.*

The day before Halloween, Paul and his team went through more checks for the Peace Conference. This time they were concentrating on and around the Conference building. Tension was high, and everyone was more than aware that no errors or slip-ups could be made. There was too much riding on this.

The aim was to create a true, far reaching United Nations; for a bond to be formed that would lead the way to peace in every country – even those which, until now, were riddled with civil war. Deep down, Paul had his doubts about peace being achieved. Human nature being what it was, there would always be some land that someone else wanted to claim, oil and minerals there for the taking, or revenge to be had from some ancient wrong-doing.

But the main thing, for him at least, was for the conference to go without a hitch, without any major disasters happening. So long as no one started threatening another country or putting sanctions on them for whatever reason, he'd be a happy chappy.

Although he hadn't felt particularly happy recently. Since the car crash, Juliet sticking knitting needles through herself and his over active imagination making him question his own rigid beliefs at times, there didn't seem a lot to be cheerful about.

Juliet was recovering, but it had been touch and go for a few days. She'd punctured her spleen and the medics had only just got the splenectomy performed in time. She'd be on drugs for the rest of her life, that was for sure – but at least she was alive.

The sight of her lying there like a life-sized voodoo doll still bugged him, and he couldn't stop thinking that her accident was kind of self-inflicted, like a spell gone wrong. As if it was a lesson not to mess with black magic. And what the hell was a crow doing in her flat?

Paul's plans were to go home to Sally tomorrow afternoon, spend a few days with her and then get back to London for the main event. He guessed he'd be back in London when the car crash couple's funeral took place. Sally would go – he guessed she would, anyway.

He was on the final lap of the train journey home when Sally called his mobile. Her picture lit up the screen. He was smiling to himself as he answered it. 'Hello gorgeous, I was just thinking about you.'

'I've got a surprise for you,' Sally said, and he could hear the excitement in her voice.

'I'm not too keen on surprises, sweetheart.'

'Don't worry, it's nothing bad. I just wanted us to have a little fun tonight when you get home.'

That would definitely be a good thing. 'Sounds good. So, what's the surprise?'

'Well if I told you …'

'I know, it wouldn't be a surprise,' he finished for her and she giggled. He loved the way she giggled. It had been a while since he'd heard that carefree tone in her voice. 'Well I should be home in about thirty minutes.' He had a thought then and it wasn't a good thought. 'Sal, there's no one there, is there? It's just you and me, right?'

'Yes, just the two of us.'

He breathed again. For a horrible moment he wondered if, in her good-natured way, she had invited Petronella Kytella for dinner. God, the thought of walking in and finding her sitting there with those cold watery eyes fixed on him sent a chill through his bones.

'Can't wait to see you,' he said, feeling a little rush of excitement through his loins. 'I've missed you.'

'Me too. See you soon, I've got to get on, things to do.'

He hung up, smiling to himself, liking the fact that she'd thought up some little surprise to brighten the evening. God, it needed brightening – five o'clock and pitch black, or it would be if you could see through the fog. He'd have to get a taxi from the station. There was no way he could find his way home through the forest in this weather.

Because of the fog the taxi took twice as long to reach home. The driver had taken his time and because of this Paul tipped him generously. 'You take care!' he told the driver.

The smells of cooking hit him the moment he walked in. The lights were off although a glimmer of orange candle-light flickered from the direction of the lounge. For a moment he was reminded of the time Sal had lain naked on the bed and he'd taken her thinking of the green-eyed blonde, or rather she'd taken him.

Dozens of orange candles flickered from every niche of the sitting room when he entered. A wood fire crackled and spat in the grate. Instantly his thoughts flew to Helena and her screaming face through the flames. On the table sat a carved pumpkin with a candle burning inside its hollow head, flames flickering through its eye sockets and gaping macabre mouth. There was a bowl with apples floating in water, and a cake with a witch on a broomstick iced in black. And Sally was dressed in a short sexy witch costume with a pointed orange hat and a green wig. She'd painted stars on her smiling face.

But her smile slid away as she looked at him and saw his expression, even though he tried his best not to show it.

'Why?' was all he could muster.

She looked helpless, tried to smile. 'Because it's Halloween. I've made us a cake and sausages and some whisky punch, it's really potent ...'

He looked incredulously at her. 'Sal, we do have some witch issues going on at the moment – Juliet ... Petronella! Have you forgotten?'

'Of course I haven't forgotten,' she snapped. 'I thought this would cheer us both up.'

'Sal, your best friend is lying in hospital after concocting a dark ritual that backfired.'

'She had an accident. She fell on her blasted knitting needles,' Sally retorted stiffly. 'And because of that it's stopped us having a bit of harmless fun?'

'Sal, Halloween is another typical American trend. Don't they realise they're celebrating something that is evil?'

She gasped. 'That's a bit over the top, isn't it?'

'It's not over the top at all,' argued Paul. 'Juliet admits to being a white witch. She attempted witchcraft and ended up almost killing herself. How do you know that every time you celebrate this kind of thing you're not doing the dark side a favour?'

She gasped. 'Now you're being completely ridiculous.'

'Look, Sal, I'm sorry, and I appreciate your efforts. I just don't like Halloween.'

'Fine!' she snapped, throwing her hat and wig onto the floor and stomping around the room, blowing out all the candles and switching on the light. She picked the pumpkin up and for a second looked like she would like to smash it over his head. Instead, she marched into the kitchen with it and tried to force it into the bin.

'Don't throw it out, Sal. You could make soup or a pie rather than waste it.'

She stormed back into the lounge, glaring at him. 'No, I couldn't!'

'Sally …' he tried to hold her, but she pushed past him in a huff. 'I'm sorry. I'm over-reacting …'

Her face crumpled but she'd dashed upstairs before her tears had time to fall. She was a long while coming back down. Paul loosened his tie, scooped up a glass of whisky punch and flopped onto the sofa. Staring into the fire he prepared himself to see Helena's face. It appeared within seconds.

Eventually, the logs burned down, and shapes dissipated. Sally came downstairs in jeans and a fluffy sweater. He thought she looked so cute even though her eyes were puffy and red.

Her voice was curt. 'You haven't got a thing against sausage batches have you?'

'Course not. I'm starving, actually,' and he raised the empty glass. 'Punch has definitely got a kick to it.' He got up, refilled his glass and poured her one. He took it through to the kitchen where she was slicing bread rolls with a vengeance. Standing behind her, he wrapped his arms around her and nuzzled her neck. 'You smell nice.'

She relaxed against him a little. 'Maybe if you talked to me more I'd understand what's going on in your head. You keep so much locked inside of you, Paul. How can I be sure I won't get it wrong again? For all I know you might have an aversion to Christmas or New Year … or the Easter bunny.'

He moved her hair, so he could press his lips to her throat. 'I love Christmas and get drunk every New Year. Bunnies are cute but not as cute as you even when you're mad as hell.'

She turned in his arms to look at him. Her gaze seemed to spear right through to his soul. 'Christmas? Do you really love Christmas? I'm okay to put a tree up and decorations?'

His eyes closed for a moment. 'I hope we do that, Sal. But if I'm honest, truly honest, I've hated Christmas ever since Helena died, and New Year and Easter and Bank Holidays and Sundays – and every damn day of the week, until you came along. I'm hoping that I'll love this Christmas and New Year, so long as you're with me. But Halloween is a different matter entirely. There's something not right about this situation, and as for that old woman … I need to find out exactly what makes her tick. A mortal soul, or a witch?'

Sally looked steadily at him. 'Paul, if you feel that she is connected with all these horrible things going on, then maybe you should tackle it on a more official basis. Because, if you are right, then she's killing people.'

'That's exactly what I'm going to do.'

She smiled and kissed his lips. 'Good. Now that we've got that sorted, can we eat?'

'Sounds good to me.'

They made love on the sofa in front of the fire. Her skin had shimmered under the flicker of firelight and her eyes had shone with love for him.

Sally went up to bed before he did. He sat finishing off the punch, watching a film on TV, relaxed and content. He was just thinking about joining Sally when the phone rang. He knew at once it wouldn't be anything good. Only bearers of bad news rang at five minutes past midnight. He considered ignoring it, he didn't want this particular bubble to burst, but it rang on, demanding to be answered.

'Hello?'

He immediately recognised the Irish accent. For a moment his hopes rose. Let the old crone be dead, please let her be dead. It somehow seemed fitting that she'd drop dead on Halloween.

The care home nurse sounded anxious and he knew at once that Petronella Kytella wasn't dead, otherwise she'd have sounded sombre. This voice was raised, frantic almost.

'We didn't know who else to ring, apart from the police of course, you being her only visitor.'

'What's happened?'

'We assumed she was in bed. But when the night nurse looked in, her bed was empty. She's nowhere to be found. We've no idea how she's got out, there's combination locks on all the doors.'

The name hadn't been mentioned, but there was no need. There was no doubt who she was talking about. 'I presume you've checked all the other rooms. She might have wandered into someone else's bedroom, or a bathroom.'

'We've checked everywhere. The police are here now with their tracker dog. It's so cold out tonight, she'll get hypothermia. She's not with you, is she? I know that's ridiculous, you wouldn't have just taken her … only you're our last resort.'

'No, we'd hardly have done that,' he answered, the very idea being preposterous. At the same time, he glanced through to the kitchen, trying to see if the bolt was drawn across the door. Although it was just as ridiculous to imagine she could have found her way here. Besides, why would she? To his dismay, the bolt wasn't drawn across.

His insides tightened. Had the door been unlocked all evening, while he was watching television, while Sal was asleep upstairs?

Cursing under his breath for letting his guard down, and striding towards the door to bolt it, he said, 'I'll keep an eye out for her, thank you for telling me.' Then as an afterthought added, 'Let me know if she turns up.'

He hung up before the nurse could say anything else and checked the lock. The key was turned, and even though he was glad about that, he still dashed upstairs to check on Sally.

There was little moonlight as the fog shrouded everything, allowing only a pale misty gleam through the window, bathing their bedroom in a strange half-light. He could make out the shape of Sally in bed, her body rising and falling slightly with each breath. Something made him step closer, he needed to check on her, make sure … make sure it was her.

Her fair cheek was against the pillow and a strand of hair coiled around her chin. He breathed normally again, feeling ridiculous for thinking that the old woman could have slipped in and somehow changed places with Sal.

A slight sound downstairs made him start. It was just the cat flap falling into place. Just Bluebell coming home. He was glad of that, she didn't want to be out on a night like tonight, especially with it being foggy and Halloween and Petronella wandering the neighbourhood.

Lying in bed, thinking rationally, he told himself that the old woman couldn't have gone far. They'd find her okay, probably in the grounds of the nursing home. Nevertheless, he couldn't sleep and eventually went back downstairs to double check the doors and windows. Bluebell ran, meowing towards him, wrapping her cold body around his ankles, tail straight as a poker, back arched, purring.

He thought about stroking her, it was unusual for her to make a fuss of him, but remembering how she'd lashed out at Sal, he decided against it. Though he did whisper kindly to her. 'Glad to be in the warm, puss? I bet you are. You didn't happen to see a crazy old woman out there, did you?'

She purred deeper and coiled herself between his legs. Paul made sure she had food in her dish and went back to bed. She obviously wasn't hungry as she followed him up to the bedroom.

Sally murmured in her sleep as he slid under the covers, she felt soft and warm and turning onto his side he wrapped his arm around her, moulding his body into hers.

The yew tree's branches scratched against the window pane, telling him something – Sal would know, she'd be able to decipher what it was saying.

His thoughts drifted to Juliet, wondering if she was out of hospital yet. He'd ring Owen tomorrow. He'd ring the old folk's home too, see if *she* was back. He hoped she was ... or that she was dead. He knew which he'd prefer but it was hardly a Christian thought. Was he Christian? He'd got the right name, which was a start. He wasn't against Christ and religion, truth was he hadn't really thought about it, but he wasn't for the darker side, that was for sure. Maybe being a Christian would be a good thing. Maybe he should ask Sal what he needed to do to become one. Believe, he guessed. Did he believe?

People, words and random thoughts drifted through his mind as consciousness battled against the onset of sleep. An image of the diminutive Father Willoughby passed through his head. The poor man would be doing a double funeral soon. Paul thought of the little wooden cross he'd carved, and as sleep finally got the better of him he wondered vaguely if it was protecting the priest from evil. Keeping him safe. He sure hoped it was.

He awoke to the feeling of hands on his groin. He didn't open his eyes but lay there, loving the sensation of being roused from sleep in such a wonderful manner. Her fingers gripped him tightly, squeezing and stroking and he groaned, loving this awakening so much. She was kneeling between his legs, playing with him now with both hands and, opening his eyes a little, he saw her shadowy form silhouetted against the grey light of the window. Her hair hung in untidy waves around her face. Slowly, she raised her face to his and their eyes met. A rush filled him. Not an excited rush. A rush of fear.

The eyes he was staring into didn't belong to his lover. They were cold eyes, filled with hatred.

His heart froze, and he sat bolt upright. There was a smell in his nostrils – burnt hair.

'Christ!'

He grabbed her hands. Shook her, shook himself. Tried to shake off this insanity. 'Sally?'

With a force he hadn't expected, she threw his hands off her, shrieking at the top of her voice and then lunged at him with fists and nails.

With a knee jerk reaction, he brought up his foot, kicking her in the chest and clean off the end of the bed.

The sudden silence rang in his ears. Sheer horror at what he'd done enveloped him. Heart thudding, he flicked on the bedside light to see where she had fallen. There was no sound, he must have hurt her, knocked her out even. He crawled to the end of the bed. 'Sally, are you okay, I'm sorry … Sal, where are you …'

With a screech, she was on his back, nails like talons tearing at his throat. The smell of burnt hair was becoming overpowering. Instinctively, he flung her over his head, slamming her into the chest of drawers, sending ornaments crashing.

Sally lay in a crumpled heap.

'My God, Sal …'

Her head twisted to look at him with eyes that still didn't belong to this face. Then, with sickening noises of bone and sinew, her body contorted, shoulders bunched around her neck.

Raising herself onto all fours she scuttled hideously towards the door like a four-legged spider, moving with such speed. She was at the top of the stairs before he could reach her.

She didn't stop, but tumbled head over heels down the staircase. Her head finally smashing onto the stone floor with a dull thud. She lay motionless except for one distorted leg twitching.

'Sal! Oh my God, Sal!'

Dashing downstairs, he saw Bluebell by the side of her, rubbing up against Sally's face. He could hear her purring.

'Bluebell! Get away from her!'

With a glance, the cat flashed him a disdainful look and shot out through the cat flap. Kneeling by Sally's crumpled body he felt for a pulse in her throat, it was weak but there.

As stillness and silence surrounded him, he realised something else – the smell of burnt hair had gone. But now the most terrible feelings of loss swept agonising over him. Feelings he knew so well from before.

For a second it was too much to bear, the pain of losing her, losing Helena. They merged, combined into one heart-stopping agonising wail of misery. And then she groaned, stirring him into action. He ran for his phone, stabbing three nines into the keypad and gabbling out that he needed an ambulance, aware it was the third time in a week he'd needed emergency services.

Sally was starting to come around. Still talking into the phone, Paul watched her, looking for any signs of her craziness. What the hell possessed her?

A chill ran through his veins.

Paramedics felt for spinal injuries, attached a neck brace and administered pain killers. Eventually they manoeuvred Sally onto a stretcher and wheeled her out to the ambulance.

Paul stood helplessly by, then realised he'd only got his briefs on and dashed upstairs to dress, ready to go with Sal in the ambulance. The paramedic wanted details of what had happened. He hesitated, not sure how much to say, but aware that they needed to know that she'd just behaved totally out of character.

As he explained he was aware his story sounded pathetic, as if he was making it up on the spot. He knew they thought he'd pushed her. They didn't say as much though, but as they drove to the hospital one of the medics mentioned the scratch at the side of his eye that was bleeding, and no doubt they'd seen the scratches on his chest and neck, too.

'You need to get those cleaned up, sir. Scratches can turn septic too easily.'

At the hospital he went over the events with medical staff, wanting them to check for a seizure, not just the physical injuries. They listened, made notes and looked at him as if he were the worst kind of villain. He half expected the police to be called in to question him.

It was almost daybreak when the hospital staff had finished assessing her. She had broken three ribs and dislocated her left elbow. To make sure there was no bleeding in the lungs or chest infection, she was going to be laid up in hospital for the best part of the week. They put her in a side ward and when the nurse finally left them alone, Sally turned tear-filled eyes towards him.

'How did I fall, Paul? Was I sleep walking again?'

He took her hand, inching his chair close to the bed. 'What do you remember, sweetheart?'

'You, kneeling beside me, and then the paramedics fussing around me.'

'What about before that?'

She stared up at the ceiling trying to recall. She smiled a tiny shy smile. 'I remember us making love on the sofa, then I went to bed. That's it really. Next thing I'm lying at the bottom of the stairs with paramedics all around me.'

He stroked her hand, thinking how small and fragile it looked between his and his heart swelled with love and protection for her. Only he hadn't protected her, and he hated himself for letting this happen.

'What?' she murmured when he didn't speak. 'I was sleep walking again, wasn't I, Paul?'

'In a way,' he agreed. 'Sal, don't you remember getting me excited in the middle of the night, in bed?'

She laughed, or tried to but her ribs were hurting too much. 'Again? But we'd only just ... you know.'

Somehow, he kept his voice light. 'Well we did.'

'No! You must have dreamed it.' She was half frowning. Then curiously she asked, 'What did we do?'

'Well I woke up feeling your hands on me, I looked down and you were kneeling between my legs.'

She gave a little gasp of outrage, clutching her ribcage with the hand that wasn't bundled into a sling. 'I did not! You were having a horny dream.'

'It was no dream, Sal,' he said, wishing he didn't have to tell her all this. 'Everything was fine until you looked me in the eyes. Then things turned pear shaped very quickly and you sort of lashed out at me.'

Her look of embarrassed amusement slipped away. She was aghast. 'I hit you?'

Paul lifted his sweater and showed her the scratches.

'Oh my God!' She struggled to sit up, to hold him. 'I did that to you? Oh my God.' She touched the dried-up blood at the side of his eye and his throat. 'And all this?'

He nodded ruefully. 'A wild banshee was nothing compared to you. I hate to use the word, but it was like you were possessed. It took all my strength to control you. It was as if you weren't you.'

'Perhaps it was some kind of seizure,' she murmured. 'They'll be doing a CT scan on me later. Perhaps they'll find something.'

'We'll see what the results show up, but I've got my own thoughts about what's going on here.'

A frown creased her forehead. 'What do you mean?'

'I'm not going into it now, Sal, it's too off-the-wall, and besides I don't have any proof. Just trust me – and let's see what the scan has to say.'

Paul stayed at her bedside until morning, until the medics had done their rounds and he'd had the opportunity to tell the doctor again that Sally had had some sort of fit, acting totally out of character. The CT scan was scheduled for later in the day.

Paul had no intention of leaving but he could see the pain killers were working and she was drifting off. She smiled dreamily at him. 'Paul, why not go home for a while, you must be exhausted.'

'I don't want to leave you.'

'Go,' she murmured. 'Only I'll have a kiss first, please.'

He relented, knowing it was the sensible thing to do. She was in the best place. The nurses would keep an eye on her. So, being careful not to put any pressure on her bruised body, he kissed her lightly on the lips. 'I'll find out when visiting hours are, and be back then.'

'Lovely. Oh, and Paul, put some food and water down for Bluebell, will you?'

'No problem.' He blew her another kiss and left.

# Chapter 21

*L*ook how pleased they are to see me. Leading me indoors, forcing weak tea down my throat. They put me in my bed. I put my hand onto hers, and my essence envelops hers. In control, we reach into Petronella's pocket and bring out the sweet mix of wolf's pane, foxglove, hemlock and deadly nightshade gathered on the way here.

*I shall show these morons how to make tea.*

*In the kitchen we make the brew. How they love their tea. They drink, their faces contort, they writhe in agony, fall to the floor, clutching their throats, gasping for breath, spewing their guts. Others run to us. We hold the carving knife in our hand, smile as they back away. We force them down the stairs. As they walk ahead of us, we stab through their backs, piercing their hearts.*

*We turn, return upstairs and check for life. Extinguish those who struggle to hang onto their pathetic existences, and we slide the blade through their scrawny skin and bones. Finally, we return to Petronella, laying on her bed. We sit. I take Petronella's hand and slip my lifeforce into her for one last time. She has served me well.*

*Standing, I place my hand around the nurse's throat, crushing her windpipe. My work here is done. Outside, the morning's air is cool and I sense my Master's pleasure in my work. How favourably he will look on me when this task is totally fulfilled.*

Paul took a taxi back to the house. The place felt desolate as he walked in through the front door, remembering, as always, to duck his head. The memory of the time he'd carried Sal over the threshold came to mind – and the searing pain that had shot through his head. He'd never found out what had caused it. A legacy from the time of his coma, he guessed ... unless someone was sticking pins into an effigy of him.

Had it been the old woman, wanting revenge for him tormenting her and killing her cat, or was that just fanciful thinking? As kids they'd thought she was a witch but if she was, why hadn't she turned him into a toad or something rather than reverting to a good old bash on the brains with a blunt instrument.

No, he hadn't been turned into a toad, although there was no getting away from it. For nine months she had turned him into a cabbage.

He put the kettle on to make himself a coffee and replenished Bluebell's food and water bowls. There was no sign of her.

He decided to give her a shout and went to unlock the back door. He stopped in mid flow – the door was already unbolted and unlocked. Yet he'd definitely locked it last night before going to bed. Maybe in the panic of Sal's accident he'd opened the door for some reason. Had the paramedics gone out that way? He didn't think so. So why was it unlocked now?

The shivers started at the nape of his neck and spread rapidly throughout his body. Had someone been in? Was someone still here?

He ran the bolt across, went silently to the kitchen drawer and took out the biggest carving knife he could find. He moved softly across the kitchen, pushing the living room door wider. Nothing seemed out of place, although had he left the cushions that way? The curtains were closed, and he crept silently towards them, half expecting to see the toes of someone's shoes poking out from beneath.

There was nothing, and he pulled the curtains back with the knife still gripped fiercely in his hand. The grey morning light brightened the room, making it feel normal. Only it wasn't normal, Sally wasn't here ... maybe someone else was.

He tiptoed towards their workroom, alert to the fact that someone could have got in to check out the security details for the

Peace Conference on his computer. His thoughts took a new turn. Had someone got in during the night, maybe injected Sally with some kind of hallucinatory drug to ensure she kept him occupied while they rifled through his computer files, downloaded anything and everything onto memory sticks and made off through the back door?

That suddenly seemed the answer, the logical explanation. He pushed open the workroom door and stood there, taking in the room, trying to see if anything had been moved, if his desk was as he'd left it. He breathed deeply like an animal trying to pick up on any unusual scents left by a stranger. But it smelt the same, that smell of leather. His computer was off. He turned it on and checked the PC's recent history, knowing what documents should be listed, half expecting to find that list to be random and wrong as if someone else had been browsing. His paranoia was really high. But it was all in order. It still didn't stop him feeling that anyone spying would have checked his file history first and made sure that it was left in the same order. He searched further back in his files but found nothing out of sequence. Going onto his emails he saw that the latest ones from his office hadn't been opened. Surely any spy or terrorist worth his salt wouldn't have been able to resist reading those. But of course they could have, and simply marked them as unread again.

He went through the rest of the house, checking every room and cupboard, the carving knife still gripped tightly in his left hand. There was no one there, and he finally had to realise that the mistake had been his. He hadn't locked up last night. Simple as that.

He put the knife back in the drawer and made himself a strong black coffee and went online. Maybe Google would know something about witches and demonic possessions. He set about finding out.

It soon became obvious that, according to folklore, witches did have powers and could harm people, in fact anything was possible, but none of it held any solid proof. He needed time to consider all this. In his practical world he dealt with problems as they came along, physical problems, not mystical spiritual stuff you couldn't get your hands on.

Deep down, he found it hard to believe these things were truly due to witchcraft, although there was certainly something unexplainable going on. Needing some fresh air, he went through to the kitchen, opened the back door and stood looking at the garden. There was a chill to the pale morning light. The grass shimmered with frosty dew and Sally's flowers and shrubs looked wilted and sad.

He called Bluebell's name twice, aware of how hollow his voice sounded in the silence. The forest was changing colour, leaves turning yellow and bronze, branches becoming skeletal. He finished his coffee, put the cup in the sink and went back outside. As he walked across the wet grass he spotted a little grey squirrel. It stopped abruptly in whatever it was doing to look at him, standing on hind legs before scampering off towards the woods. It was the same direction he was heading in. He didn't know if he was going to do any woodcarving, maybe it would relax him.

He entered the barn, immediately breathing in the familiar scent of cut wood. As his eyes fell on the axe on the far wall, he knew why he'd come down here. It would make an ideal deterrent against intruders. He strode down the centre of the barn and lifted the axe from where it hung, surprised that it seemed heavier than usual. Maybe he was more tired than he thought. In the past, when he'd regularly carried it into the forest, he'd managed to hold it in one hand or rest it easily over his shoulder. Now it felt its weight, now it took both hands to heave it down and then it slumped with a thud on the floor.

It was unbelievably heavy. Perhaps this fatigue was down to his lack of sleep – and the mental anguish of all that had gone on. He heaved it up into both hands, aware of the pull to his shoulders as if his arms were being dragged from their sockets because of its weight.

He turned back towards the barn door, determined that he'd get the blasted thing back to the house if it killed him. This was insane, he could carry the axe *and* a lump of oak half a mile, why the hell couldn't he even drag the axe a few paltry steps now?

But then he saw what was sitting in the corner behind the open barn door.

He took a sharp intake of breath. All he could do was stand rigid, heart banging against his ribcage, staring at her – the old woman from the nursing home.

The witch.

Petronella Kytella sat upright against the wall, legs spread wide, feet turned upwards, head slumped like a marionette waiting for someone to pull the strings and bring her dancing back to life.

'What the hell ...' Paul could barely get the words out. 'What the hell are you doing here?'

Without a word, without a sound, she looked up at him, her eyes peering through her bedraggled hair, piecing his. He knew straight away. These were the eyes that had looked at him last night, in his bed.

The hairs stood up on the back of his neck. 'Explain yourself!'

She started to cough, a choking, rasping sound, but then the tone changed, turning into a cackle of laughter – a laugh of pure evil.

He took a step backwards as she started to rise, not using her hands to push herself upwards, just a slow straightening of her crooked body, until she was standing, facing him. As tall as him. His hands tightened around the axe, ready to cleave her in half if she came at him.

Her laughter stopped as suddenly as it had started. And she spoke. 'Now, do you see what you are dealing with?'

With a flick of her bony hand the axe flew out of his grasp, spinning across the barn floor, slamming against the far wall.

'What the ...'

'Paul Christian, everything in your life is soon to change.'

'Why are you doing this?'

Her face contorted. 'Revenge. You burn Theron, my cat, I burn your wife.'

'My wife?' He staggered. The pain was back. Searing pain shooting like needles through his skull.

'Pretty Helena, how she squealed.'

Fingers pressed against his temples, he tried to stem the pain.

'I have watched you for a long, long time, Paul Christian. 'You can never escape me. You will soon be dancing to my tune.'

He struggled to stay coherent. 'All because of your cat, all those years ago?'

Her mouth contorted to a sneer. 'You have no idea what a witch's cat means to her.'

Fighting back the pain, he demanded, 'Who the hell are you?'

'What you see before you, is not what you think. I am not Petronella. I just live in her.'

'Talk sense, woman.'

'The next time you see this body, it will be dead.'

Pain or no pain, Paul moved swiftly, throwing himself towards the axe. He lifted it easily, turned back with it raised above his head. 'You need certifying ...'

The space where she stood was empty.

Petronella, or whoever it was, had gone.


*Time to take back what is mine. She will come to me. I knock, and step back five paces. The door opens.*

*'Can you help me?' I plead in the tone these humans cannot resist. 'I don't feel well.'*

*How anxious she looks. She does not remember. My visits brought me here with the birds, not as a pathetic old woman. I reach out to her. She runs swiftly to me, takes hold of my trembling hands.*

*I look into her eyes. 'I have need of you.'*

*My lifeforce slips into this young host, there is no resistance. Mind and body, I possess them both.*

*From behind vivid green eyes I see Petronella Kytella crumple to her knees, she falls flat to the ground. I roll her onto her back with my foot and look into the face I have possessed for so many years.*

*'Go Petronella! You are finally free to die.'*

Petronella, wife and mother, felt the spirit of Lamia leave her body for the final time. She would not return, she had given her permission to die. Joy filled Petronella's heart as the black demonic possession bade her farewell.

Now she breathed in the fresh, cold air as she lay on the soft earth, gazing up at the blue sky. She could smell the sweetness of the grass, hear the rustle of leaves and the sound of birdsong. Free at last.

Looking up, clouds parted, sunlight shone brilliantly through and she saw people reaching down to her – her son, her husband, her mother and father …

Happiness flooded through her aged body, and taking one final breath, Petronella departed this earth in peace.

# Chapter 22

Paul could think of only one place she might go – back to the care home. Grabbing the axe which amazingly seemed to be back to its normal weight, he ran to where Sally had parked her car. It would normally take twenty minutes to get there but he was going to do it in a lot less time than that.

Lights were on behind the closed curtains. He rang the bell and banged on the door, no one came. A sense of foreboding forced his hand. He ran back for the axe and slammed it straight through the glass panel and forced his way in.

With no one at the desk, he recalled the combination code and dashed through to the sitting room. There was no sound, and no movement. But there was a stench of vomit and a metallic smell which could only mean one thing.

Taking in the scene his urgency dissipated and an intense veil of sorrow settled over him. Paul walked softly towards the old man sitting in the nearest chair. His head was bowed, almost as if he were praying. He recognised the dressing gown as the old wandering guy. Paul checked for a pulse, then realised there'd hardly be one after being stabbed clean through the heart.

As he reached for his phone he checked the old lady in the next seat. Vomit had pooled in her lap along with her false teeth.

Sickened, he summoned the police, hardly able to believe he was saying 'massacre' and 'care home' in the same breath. Systematically, he checked for life, finding none. Even the staff, all brutally stabbed to death.

He looked for Petronella, going from bedroom to bedroom, axe in hand. There was no sign of her, but he did find the Irish nurse.

She was slumped backwards in a chair by a bed, her throat crushed and all but ripped out.

Anger raged. He guessed where Petronella had gone. The place of so many of his childhood fears. He raced back to his car; he would explain his absence to the police later. Right now, she needed to be found before she killed anyone else.

With the tyres screaming, he tore around the country lanes, finally pulling up as close to the witch's cottage as he could. Axe in hand, he ran swiftly through the forest, the morning light glimmering through the trees.

As always, a crow was hunched up on the roof. But there was also something else visible. Someone lying on the path.

Even before reaching her, he knew it was Petronella. He stood over the prostrate body. She lay flat on her back, eyes staring blindly up to the sky. As dead as she had predicted.

Fearing for the woman inside, he hammered on the door until it was opened.

A sleepy-looking blonde frowned at him. 'Hello?'

'Did you know there's a body lying out here? You haven't called the police?'

'A body …' she peered outside and clutched her dressing gown tightly. 'Oh, my goodness! We need to call an ambulance.'

'It's a bit late for that. Call the police,' said Paul. He looked steadily at her. 'So, she didn't knock your door, or speak to you?'

'No, I never knew she was there. I was in bed till you knocked. I wonder how long she's been there. I wonder who she is, anyway?'

'Call the police and I'll explain it to you.'

'Yes, of course. Come in, won't you.'

As she spoke on the phone, Paul gazed around the cottage – the place of his childhood nightmares. Now it held no fears. It was bright and modern, and perfectly renovated.

'They'll be here as quickly as they can.' She smiled at him. 'Can I make you a coffee or tea?'

'Coffee, thank you. Black, no sugar.'

She went through to the tiny kitchen. 'This probably isn't the best time to be holding a conversation, but we may as well introduce ourselves. I'm Diane Lewis.'

The name rang a bell. 'Paul Christian.'

'Yes, I remember you from when your friend accused me of sleeping with her man, but I've also seen you on the London train now and again. I don't think you've noticed me, though.'

That surprised him, as he'd thought he'd easily have spotted her in a crowd. 'So, what do you do in London?'

She poked her head around the door. 'I'm an interpreter. I'm involved in the Peace Conference ...'

'You're kidding!' he said, recognising the name now from one of his lists. 'That's my line of work, too.'

Her green eyes widened. 'My goodness, what a small world. What do you do?'

'Oh, I'm just there to keep the wheels running smoothly.'

'Ah,' she said knowingly. 'Something important, then.'

Paul smiled.

They'd barely taken a sip of coffee when the police arrived. The area was swiftly cordoned off, and Paul sat down with an officer to make a statement. Or rather tell them as much as they needed to know.

He'd no doubt that there'd be a few raised eyebrows if he started talking about witches and witchcraft. So he told them instead of how Petronella had turned up at his barn and talked about dying. He'd wanted to drive her back to the care home only she'd disappeared when he'd turned his back. So, he'd driven to the home, concerned about the old dear's state of mind. He'd had no option but to break in.

Finding so many people dead – and no sign of Petronella – Paul explained why he hadn't waited around after calling the police. Obviously, she'd killed everyone before turning up at his barn. He explained that he'd needed to find her before she killed anyone else. The only other place he could think of where she might go was back to her former home. His assumptions had been correct.

It was late afternoon by the time he left the police station. He badly needed to see Sally – and he'd forgotten how hungry he was. He grabbed a quick sandwich from a local shop and drove to the hospital. The axe in the boot of Sally's car.

She wasn't in the side room. Wasting no time, he checked with the duty nurse as to where Sally Knightly had been moved to.

'We've put her in a six-bedder,' said the nurse, pointing along the corridor. 'A friend of hers had been admitted after an accident, so we put them together. Good company for each other!'

'Juliet, of course!' With everything happening he'd forgotten she was still in hospital.

Juliet was in the first bed. Her cheeks ruddy as if she'd been pumped full of fresh blood – which she had been. Four pints of it. Seeing him, a tear rolled down her cheek.

Sally was in the next bed, quite pale but sitting up. She nodded her head towards her friend, indicating he needed to speak to her first. He obliged, taking Juliet's hands in his.

She clung to him. 'I should have been dead. You stopped me from bleeding to death, you and Sally. I'll never be able to thank you both enough.'

'Owen too. He did his bit, don't forget that, Juliet. And if you're ever in any doubt that he doesn't love you, you should have seen the state he was in, seeing you like that.'

'Yes, I gather,' she said, lowering her eyes.'

'So, what happened?' Paul asked, still able to picture her lying there like her voodoo doll. 'I never thought knitting carried a health warning!'

'I tripped.'

'On what?'

'I don't know, I'm just clumsy, I suppose.'

Paul glanced at Sally, willing her not say anything. 'Juliet, this may sound an odd question, but you didn't happen to see a bird sitting on the windowsill or anything before your accident?'

She stared at him. 'Now you mention it, I do remember something … I didn't see a bird, but I heard a flapping sound when I hit the floor. What made you ask me that?'

Paul and Sally exchanged glances.

'What?' Juliet puzzled.

'Well,' began Sally. 'When I found you, I swear I saw a bird flying out of your window.'

'What sort of bird?'

'A crow.'

Juliet visibly swayed. 'My God. The harbinger of death.'

Sally gasped. 'Juliet, don't. That's the just myth and nonsense.'

She almost smiled. 'It's not far wrong though, it is? I would have died if you hadn't found me.'

Paul thought about the crow still perched on the old cottage. Petronella had certainly brought death to the poor souls at the nursing home. He dreaded having to give Sal and Juliet more distressing news. The only good thing being that Petronella was dead and couldn't do any more harm.

He moved to Sally's bedside, and kissed her. Looking at Juliet he asked, 'So what is it with crows, then?'

Juliet sighed. 'They've always been linked with bad situations, deaths and such. They even say witches could take over the creature's body to escape nasty situations.'

Paul wished he'd never asked. The possibility of Petronella's black soul having gone into a bird was an uncomfortable thought. And were the birds the only option?

'Paul …' Sally touched his hand. 'What are you thinking?'

He sat on the edge of her bed. 'I have to tell you something. I only wish I didn't have to. It's about Petronella – she's dead, by the way.'

'Oh no!'

'And she didn't go alone. Sal, I was right in thinking she was dangerous.'

Both women sat open mouthed as he related what had gone on. And then they wept, both knowing some of the nurses and old folk who had been slaughtered at Petronella's hand.

It was hard saying goodbye to Sally and leaving her behind in hospital, although he knew it was the best place for her right now. He learned that results of her scan hadn't shown up anything untoward and she hadn't had any other peculiar turns, but still he was glad she was being kept under observation for a few more days at least. She was still tearful when the time came for him to go. 'I wish you didn't have to leave.'

'You just get yourself better.'

'I'll be saying my prayers for you. Take care, won't you? Watch out for bombs and booby-trapped cars.'

'Sal, the amount of security we've laid on is unbelievable. A sewer rat won't be able to twitch its whiskers without us knowing about it.'

She clung to him, reluctant to let him go. 'I just hate the thought of all those top people all in one place, it's just asking for some lunatic to cause trouble.'

He kissed her. The politics of his job never worried him unduly. And Petronella was the only lunatic he knew, and she was dead. Things were looking brighter.


Back home, he packed for his stay in London. After all that had gone on, he was quite amazed that he'd remembered the bust. It seemed so paltry compared to everything that had happened. Nevertheless, he fetched it from the barn, returning the axe to its place at the same time. He tried not to shudder as he glanced at the place he'd found Petronella Kytella waiting for him.

After locking the place securely, he put down food and water for Bluebell and dug out an old hat box that he'd spotted on top of Sal's wardrobe. The bust fitted perfectly. It would bring a bit of humour to the conference, if nothing else.

He took the train to London on the Sunday evening, finding himself keeping an eye out for Diane Lewis. Clearly, she hadn't taken the same train as him.

Three hours later he was in his hotel room. And by seven the next morning he was walking along by the Thames towards work.

It wasn't the quickest route, but he enjoyed the walk. This morning proved a bit more awkward carrying a briefcase and a hat box.

Crossing the Lambeth Bridge, Thames House loomed ahead, a huge, imposing, grey stone building with an obviously noticeable police presence around it today. In fact, there were armed police on every corner, which was good, and how it was meant to be. The Peace Conference had meant everyone was on high alert in every branch of security.

Once inside the building he passed through security as usual. He'd wondered if he'd be questioned about what was in the hat box. But his position here meant that no one stopped and questioned him. His pass allowed him through, and the bust didn't set off any alarms. But then why should it? It was just a lump of wood. It wasn't radioactive and didn't contain anything dangerous.

After taking the lift he passed the Chief's office, turned the corner and entered his own office. He was first in, and as his colleagues turned up for work they all wanted to know how Sally was. He'd had no option but to let Daniel Rake know of her accident, although he kept the details to a minimum. He'd informed him about the massacre at the care home and finding the body of Petronella Kytella who was presumed to have murdered everyone. The reason for her death was yet to be confirmed.

Paul soon realised that his colleagues were useless at keeping secrets, unless they were State secrets, as one by one, like Chinese whispers, everyone he knew popped by to ask how Sally was.

'I thought we were in the security business,' Paul remarked jovially after he'd assured the latest caller that Sally was well on the mend. 'Talk about hearing it on the grapevine!'

Agents Fitzpatrick and Brooke were still with Daniel Rake in his office, drinking coffee, when Paul lifted out the bubble wrapped bust and placed it on his desk. He sat back, arms folded, awaiting their reaction.

Rake picked it up, turning it in hands. 'I am seriously impressed, Paul. I think the president is going to love this. I told you we'd got the okay for it, didn't I? So long as the Yanks are happy. They'll probably want to have a look at it.'

'Let's hope there aren't any objections,' said Paul with a wry smile. 'Sally says she's not having a bust of President Howard on her mantlepiece!'

There was knock at the door, and a certain green-eyed blonde poked her head around.

'Diane ... what a surprise. Come on in.'

He introduced her to Daniel, noticing how all the guys' eyes lit up. 'This is Diane Lewis, who as well as being an interpreter here, is also my neighbour ... well, pretty much.'

The way they almost fell over each other to shake her hand made Paul smile to himself.

Her eyes fell on the bust. 'Wow. That is a good likeness. Someone's a fan of the President.'

'This is Paul's creation,' said Rake. 'Very soon to be presented to the big man himself, and probably in front of all the other delegates at the end of the Conference. Sorry Paul, I haven't had chance to tell you that, yet.'

'No pressure, then!'

Diane moved towards the bust. 'May I?'

'Help yourself,' said Paul.

She ran her hand down the President's cheek in almost a sensual caress. 'It's beautifully carved, so smooth ... Oh!'

Paul immediately thought she'd got a splinter, but it seemed more than that. Her legs seemed to buckle slightly, making her grip the edge of the desk.

Paul was first to catch hold of her, while Fitzpatrick grabbed a chair for her to sit back into. 'Are you okay?'

She rested her head in her hands for a moment. 'Sorry, I just went a bit woozy. That'll teach me to skip breakfast.'

'Can I get you a glass of water?' asked Paul.

She glanced up at him and smiled vaguely. 'No, I'm fine now. I'd better get on. I just wanted to pop by and say hello.'

'I'm glad you did,' said Paul. And as she left, he saw how Rake raised one eyebrow.

'What?' Paul mused. 'She's just a neighbour.'

# Chapter 23

The day before the Peace Conference began, a blanket of fog swirled over the Thames, making Paul think of the pea-soupers from the last century. It was unusually cold too, more like December than November and that made him think of Christmas. His first Christmas with Sally was going to be perfect. He'd make sure of it.

Now at 9.30am he and Daniel Rake were shadowing the US President's car as it journeyed through London's streets after landing at the airport a short while earlier. He watched the bulletproof limousine cruise along ahead of them, unhindered and mainly unobserved, although the media were out in full.

Paul had been among the welcoming party for the American VIPs at the airport, and seeing the President in the flesh made him realise just how precise his wood carving really was.

Arrivals went on throughout the day with dignitaries, Heads of State, presidents and prime ministers – and some whom until today, Paul would have labelled as terrorists, all making their way into the capital in readiness for the biggest Peace Conference the world had ever seen.

Everyone was on high alert, Paul knew their own armed officers were on every street and staked out at every vantage point. Tension was so acute you could practically taste it. The whole atmosphere was brittle.

For sure, Paul would be glad when the whole thing was over and World War Three hadn't been triggered by some random remark or terrorist act.

Everyone from the Chief of Defence down had been hoping their foreign guests would simply stay put in their hotels until the start of the conference tomorrow, but some of them wanted to see the sights of London, and created havoc as they changed their schedules and went to the London Eye, Tower Bridge, Big Ben and Soho.

'Happy holidays!' Paul groaned to Daniel Rake, as they quelled a small riot when one Middle Eastern diplomat tried to queue jump at the London Eye.

'Well, would you want to come all this way and *not* see the London Eye?' Daniel Rake remarked with a wry smile.

It was the first light hearted moment of the day, and Paul found himself feeling vaguely optimistic that this Conference was actually going to go off without any trouble.

## 7 November 2018

Security was immense for the conference, and the procedures they'd put in motion went without a hitch. Foreign dignitaries were brought along to the dedicated conference centre smoothly and without fuss. When every single one of them had taken their seats in the plush semi-circular room and the talks got underway, minders and the personal security staff of the VIPs could stand down. One by one they descended into the conference centre's green lounge, set aside especially for them.

For Paul this proved to be the best moment of the day. If any of the visitors were feeling any distrust, it didn't show, and there was plenty of light-hearted banter going on, even though the language was a barrier in some cases. He half hoped that Diane Lewis would pop by and help with some interpreting. She was obviously being utilised elsewhere.

Over lunch he chatted to one of the American President's agents, a guy named Carter who he'd spoken to over the phone on a number of occasions.

'I hear you've made President Howard a bust,' the burly 22-stone guy said. 'He's looking forward to receiving it. And don't be surprised if he calls you personally. He's an amiable guy, he'll probably want to shake your hand.'

'I just hope he likes it,' said Paul, a twinge of doubt over his craftsmanship setting in.

'Sure he will,' said Carter. 'Now can I get another cup of English tea? It's damn good!'

Day two went perfectly, then at 4am on the Friday morning – the final day of the Conference – Paul's mobile rang. Through bleary eyes he saw Sally's face light up on the little screen.

'Sal! Are you okay?'

Her voice whispered back, and he knew she was talking from her hospital bed and trying not to wake anyone. 'I'm fine, I just wanted to hear your voice and I thought this was the best time to catch you not working.'

He relaxed back onto his pillow and closed his eyes, glad to hear her voice. 'Good thinking, though I'm on call if anything kicks off.'

'How's it going?'

'Good … really good. Surprisingly good, actually. Final day of talks coming up and no-one's shot anyone yet.'

'Oh, don't say that, Paul. It worries me to death. All those important people in the one place. It's a terrorist's dream.'

He smiled through the darkness of his room. 'Well that's what we're hoping to combat. If the bods can get everyone singing from the same hymn sheet, so to speak, there won't be any more terrorism.'

'It's such a high improbable hope, though.'

'I know,' agreed Paul. 'We all know that, but at least everyone is trying.'

She fell silent for a moment, and when she spoke there was a tremor in her voice. 'Paul, I miss you.'

'I miss you too, Sal.' He sucked in a deep breath. What he'd just said was a gross understatement. He ached to see her again, to hold her close, kiss her, make love to her. And then because there was no point in winding himself up, as it would be days yet before he could see her again, he asked, 'How are you feeling?'

She gave a sort of quiet laugh in return before answering. 'I'm okay, apart from missing you and being bored out of my mind just lying in bed all day. I need to be back at work. I have bags to make! I just hope they discharge me soon.'

'Don't rush things, Sal. Make sure you're out of the woods.'

'I was hoping to be home for the Clarkes' funeral ...'

Images of Mrs Clark waving as they slammed into the brick wall jumped back into his head. 'Is that a good idea, Sal? Haven't you been through enough, recently?'

'I feel I should. I knew them ...' She broke off in mid-sentence and fell silent for a moment. 'Actually, Juliet said something today which was really bizarre.'

'Well that doesn't surprise me, but go on, what did she say?'

Sally hesitated again. 'Don't take this the wrong way, Paul, but there's no denying it.'

'What? Come on Sal, spill the beans, what's she been saying now?'

'Well, she just made the point that Mrs Scott, the doctor's wife, bought one of your carvings – the horse, and the Clarkes bought your clogs ... and, well, they're all dead.'

'Sal, they've probably all bought a loaf of bread and a pound of pork sausages from the local butcher, too.' As he spoke a nagging worry he'd had for some time reared its head. Now hearing it from Sally and Juliet gave him the uncomfortable feeling that the notion wasn't as insane as he'd thought. There was no point in worrying Sally any more than she was already. 'It's a coincidence, nothing more. And don't let Juliet's babblings bother you. Now get some sleep. I'll see you soon.'

'Yes, see you soon. Oh, and Paul ... don't let your guard down.'

The day's proceedings went smoothly. Rake had kept him up to scratch with all that had gone on, and it sounded promising with agreements made between different countries, reductions in arms between some of the more powerful nations and more co-operation between Governments to stop terrorist activities. There could be no denying, even from the most politically cynical of folk, that this had been a worthwhile event. Anything that brought peace to this world had to be good.

Late afternoon on the Friday, Rake's secretary came and summoned Paul from the green room. 'Would you like to come through? It's the farewell speeches now, and Daniel wants you ready to present the bust to President Howard.'

He got to his feet. 'Okay, only I haven't seen it since they took it away for scanning.'

'It's sitting on a table outside the conference room.' She smiled. 'Ready?'

'As I ever will be.'

He followed her along the corridor. True enough, the bust was on a side table by the main doors. 'Go in, Paul, and I'll hand you the bust once Daniel's announced it.'

A twinge of nerves hit him. If the President hated it, he was in deep shit.

He was familiar with the Conference Room. Over the last few weeks he'd grown accustomed to every nook and cranny, every escape exit, fire alarm, waste paper bin and fire extinguisher. The sight of it now as he slipped through the door, filled with fifty foreign diplomats, made him feel a sense of pride for a job well done.

The Prime Minister was addressing the room, thanking them all, and congratulating them on the success of the conference. She glanced over at Paul. 'Ah yes, ladies and gentlemen I am sure that had there been more time, our Head of Security - Paul Christian - would have carved a figurine of each and every one of you. And I admit I'm rather jealous that he didn't do one of me!' Her words brought a ripple of laughter from the seated VIPs. 'Paul, do please bring in the wonderful carving you've made. President Howard, this is hand-crafted in English oak and our gift to you.'

The door behind him opened, and the bust was passed through to him. Slightly embarrassed, Paul held it in both hands, with the face looking towards the President and the delegates.

The President's face broke into a smile as Paul approached. 'Mr Christian, I want to say a mighty big thank you. It's a real neat piece of woodwork. I reckon you could take a few orders from our honoured visitors here and earn yourself a dollar or two.'

Everyone laughed. Paul allowed himself a smile and a quiet, 'Thank you, Sir.'

The President reached out, shook Paul's hand and accepted the bust. He raised it above his head, turning the carving to show everyone.

At that moment, Paul saw the carved face – the face that he had so delicately chiselled and honed.

His insides dropped, as if someone had pulled the lavatory chain and every part of his innards were heading south. Alarm bells jangled in his skull and a sudden rush of bile surged up his throat. There was an expression on that chunk of wood that he hadn't carved.

He hadn't put hate in those wooden eyes. He hadn't created that demonic look – that expression of pure malicious evil. He'd done none of that, but there it was, for all the world to see.

Before he could move, before he could grab the bust back, there was a tremendous ear-shattering noise. The sound of a hand clap only amplified a hundred times louder. His ears rang as splinters shot out across the room, embedding themselves into the shocked diplomats.

With a cry, the President dropped the remnants of the bust.

Realisation dawned. Paul's brain went into a spin. Petronella was in the bust. He saw that now. It was like before, with the ugly carving. She was in them all; the reclining naked figure, the clogs the Clarks bought before slamming their car into a brick wall; the horse the doctor's wife had bought before falling downstairs and breaking her neck. Petronella Kytella had poisoned them all. What Sally had said last night was right. God, what had he created?

Hosts for witchcraft - so she could travel, reach out, wreak havoc? Petronella Kytella was far from dead.

Most of the VIPs had dived for cover, while security officers came racing in from all directions. What was left of the bust lay on the floor, sneering up at him.

The evil was still there, inside it. He moved swiftly not knowing what it would do next. As he picked it up from the floor a shock jolted his body.

Confusion swamped as a sensation of losing control washed over him. It was suddenly impossible to think straight. He struggled to keep hold of reality – his mind tumbling.

But he saw a waste paper bin and dropped the bust into it. Then, holding the bin at arm's length, he made for the exit looking as if he was holding a bomb in a bucket of sand. And of course, it was a bomb, a bomb powered by evil and hatred that had burst upon the world. And it was all his doing. She'd manipulated him. Worked him like a puppet.

He ran with it, down one corridor, along another. Every step was like wading in thick mud and with every step he felt he was losing the battle for control of his thoughts. Turning a corner, he saw through blurred eyes Daniel Rake and half a dozen security men staring at him. Their guns were drawn, and pointed in his direction.

He fell to his knees. Blackness and oblivion enveloping him.

# Chapter 24

*S*plinters *pierce their pathetic bodies, bringing confusion and bad judgement. I am content with my deceit. And now I lay quietly within his mind, watching, listening, giving him back some control – for now.*

The mugginess in Paul's head was starting to clear, and with clarity arose reality. He now knew, without a doubt, that it *was* witchcraft that had caused all of the mayhem. He had never believed in it, but now he saw there could be no other explanation and he felt a sudden jolt of empathy for all the people who had been affected by witchcraft and never been believed. Now it was his turn. No one was going to believe what he had to tell them, that it was all Petronella's work – her and the carvings. She'd manipulated him. To what ends he didn't know.

Through the carvings, even the fallen oak, she'd provided the utensils and given him the skills to make objects that she could somehow inhabit, and infect those who handled them, causing pure destruction.

Had it stemmed from when he was a kid, and her cat had got burnt? Could her anger have lasted all these years?

And she'd spoken about Helena. Had she been manipulative in that, too? His thoughts shot back to Helena crashing into the tanker. There had been a cat in that cabin. His head throbbed with anger and rage. Why hadn't he seen all this? Yet, how could he? And now who in their right mind was going to believe him?

Looking around his ward, he saw Agent Fitzpatrick seated on a chair by the door, staring at him. 'Sir,' he murmured as their eyes met. And when the door opened a moment later, and Daniel Rake came in with two coffees, he glimpsed Agent Brooke standing guard outside.

'You're looking a bit more with it, Paul,' Daniel said, sitting down next to his bed. 'Here, drink this.'

Paul took the paper cup. 'Thanks.'

'You've been rambling, Paul. Are you up to explaining what happened? We aren't accusing you of anything, and thankfully no one was seriously hurt.'

'Thank God for that.'

'We've run tests on that bust,' Rake continued. 'It's nothing but a piece of oak, no explosive devices, no accelerants, no poison on those splinters. No rational explanation at all for what it did.'

Paul looked steadily at Rake. 'It was witchcraft.'

Rake spluttered out a mouthful of coffee. 'What!' He glanced at Fitzpatrick who had raised an eyebrow.

'I know you're not going to believe me. But it was her, that damn witch.'

'A witch?' Rake repeated. 'Paul, make some sense, will you?'

Paul sat up in bed. There were dressings on his hands from where the splinters had punctured his skin. 'I know you're going to struggle with this, but what I'm telling you is true. I guarantee there will be something major behind this, and it won't be good. This whole thing is witchcraft.'

Fitzpatrick gave a chuckle of laughter.

'I thought she was dead,' Paul went on. 'But she's not. She's alive somehow, and still manipulating and killing.'

'No one died, Paul.'

'I'm not talking about the conference. I mean the care home, the couple in the car, the doctor's wife, Sally, Juliet, the knitting needles. Don't you see, it's all down to her.'

Rake put a hand on his shoulder. 'Okay, then who is this person? What's her name? We'll check her out.'

Paul stared at him. 'You can't check her out, she's dead. That's how devious she is. Her name was Petronella Kytella, and all her medical records will be at Oakwoods Residential Home – where she massacred everyone.'

Rake looked steadily at him. 'Paul, I don't know about this witch situation but if she's been active as a terrorist, we need to know about her to see if anybody else is involved.'

'Do that,' said Paul, 'but you're barking up the wrong tree. She's got supernatural powers, Daniel. She's a fucking witch!'

'She's a murderer, Paul, nothing more.' said Rake calmly, 'She killed over 30 people at the care home, but she's not some sort of supernatural being that can do hocus pocus spells. That's crap and doesn't exist.'

'That's what I thought, but believe me, Daniel, she can do all that kind of shit. God knows what she's capable of.'

'But she's dead. You found her body, which is now on a slab in the mortuary.'

'I know all that,' he agreed. 'But I'm telling you she was in that bust just before it exploded, or however you want to phrase it. I saw the evil, only it was too late to do anything about it.'

'Paul, you're talking madness. She was a crazy old woman who knew she was dying and wanted to take a few dozen with her.'

'If only it was that simple. This goes far back …'

'Paul, look, I honestly think you're stressed. Maybe even – I don't like to suggest this – but maybe having some kind of breakdown.'

'I'm not mad, Daniel.' He spoke swiftly. 'She said something about Helena, I think she orchestrated Helena's death. That tanker went out of control because the driver had a cat in the cab. Cat's go wild and attack their owners sometimes, I've seen it with Bluebell …'

He stopped in mid-sentence. Icy cold prickles breaking out all over his skin. 'Bluebell …'

There had always been creatures around him; animals, birds. There was the mouse when Sally had behaved so out of character, and Bluebell, coming and going as she pleased. Had she brought Petronella's spirit with her, infecting him, infecting Sally. The night she went crazy – was that all due to Petronella?

'Paul, I'm talking to you.'

He swung his legs out of bed. It wasn't just wood carvings she transported her evil through, it was animals and birds. 'I need to get out of here.'

'You're going nowhere for now,' Rake said, pushing him back on the bed. 'I'm going to ask the nurse to sedate you. And we'll see about more tests … see if anything weird is going on in that brain of yours. You're having a scan tomorrow, full body; your head, your heart, your feet, every damn where. You're my top man, Paul, I don't like to see you like this. If there's anything in you, hallucinatory drugs, anything, we're going to sort it. And in the meantime Fitzpatrick will take over. You know he's a good man.'

Paul struggled against Daniel Rake, desperate to be back on his feet. Sally could be in danger. He needed to warn her.

Fitzpatrick came and stood next to Rake. 'Take it easy, sir.'

There was no convincing them, Paul saw that, and the last thing he wanted was to be sedated. He fell back against his pillow. 'Okay, I'll stay put. No need for any sedation.'

Rake patted his shoulder. 'Okay, but we'll arrange those tests. And then, my friend, you can take some time off and recuperate.'

'So, I'm not being arrested for terrorism with the exploding bust?'

'No. Apart from a few punctures from splinters – well quite a few – there were no serious injuries. But no one escaped those flying bits of wood; not the PM, President Howard, everyone got hit, but basically they've all just suffered from very minor scratches. It's nothing too disastrous. Naturally, we are hoping this doesn't cause a diplomatic incident and we've assured everyone that we're in the process of getting to the bottom of this. And we have to be showing we're giving you the third degree. You understand that?'

Paul nodded. There was no point in arguing. But deep down he knew they were wrong. This would be disastrous and somehow he had to make them believe him.

A whole week in hospital, and having undergone every kind of test imaginable – from psychological to a polygraph - nothing untoward was found, physically or mentally, within Paul. There was no reason for him to be held any longer. But returning to work was temporarily out of the question. Daniel Rake recommended home rest. And Paul couldn't wait to get his and Sally's life back on track.

He'd managed only one phone call to her, which was observed by Fitzpatrick. He'd had his orders to keep everything very basic, and not to start talking in spiritual or demonic terms. He didn't argue. No point in frightening Sally.

She was still in hospital – both her and Juliet. Sally burst into tears when he walked into their ward.

'What happened, Paul?' Sally cried, reaching out to him. 'I've been trying to call you …'

'It's okay, Sal,' he lied, not wanting to talk about witchcraft. 'Things have kicked off at work. There's things I need to do. I just wanted to see you first.'

She clung onto him. 'What sort of things?'

'Nothing for you to worry about.'

'Stop saying that, will you. I'm worried sick. I heard something on the news about an explosion at the Peace Conference. They mentioned a gift for the President being booby trapped. Paul, were they talking about the bust?'

'First of all, there was no explosion, but there was something wrong with the wood I was using.' He turned to Juliet. 'Juliet, I need the keys to your shop, so I can get all the carvings back. I can't explain any more than that. Just trust me, okay?'

'I don't have my keys, Paul. I could ring Owen and get him to collect the carvings and bring them to the cottage.'

'Tell him not to touch them, wear thick gloves.' He hadn't any idea whether that would make any difference. Hell, he didn't even know if they were infected. But he couldn't risk it.

He thanked Juliet and kissed Sally goodbye, desperate to reach Father Willoughby to make sure all was well with him. He'd given him the cross, and he just prayed that wasn't cursed as well.

'You're going right now?' Sally asked, dismayed. 'The doctors said I should be allowed home today. Will you come and pick me up?'

'Sal, I don't know how the day is going to go. Get a taxi, would you? I'll see you back home.'

As he drove, dream-like thoughts flitted through his head, strange images, like memories, but not *his* memories. He shook his head, trying to clear his brain, but flashes skimmed like old-fashioned film flitting through his brain. The church, Father Willoughby, a tin of rat poison ...

He almost careered off the road. What the hell was this – a premonition? He turned the car towards the church and rammed his foot hard down on the accelerator.

A stream of cars were parked along the kerbside. Mass was in full swing. He screeched to a halt, stumbling as he raced up to the closed church door. His legs felt weak suddenly, it was an effort to run. Fear, he guessed, not knowing what to expect, dreading walking into another massacre like in the care home. He could just imagine the congregation sitting rigid in the pews; sick, poisoned, dead. The old myth sprang into his head, and he could suddenly see clear as day, men, women, children, screaming, clawing at their throats as the poisoned hosts entered their bodies.

'No!' he threw himself against the church door. It hit the inside wall with a deafening crash. The congregation turned to look accusingly at him. Father Willoughby had the chalice in his hands, and the first few rows of people were on their feet, queuing to receive Holy Communion.

A sharp pain suddenly shot through Paul's head. 'Jesus!' he cried clutching his head as he stumbled forward. Father Willoughby's face paled at the sight of him. Through blurred eyes he saw the little priest step towards him.

Blinding pain now shot through every part of his body as if he was being stabbed by a hundred daggers from the inside out.

'Poisoned ...' Paul blurted out. 'Don't ...'

Paul summoned all of his energy to knock the chalice from the priest's hand, scattering the hosts across the marble floor. Someone screamed. People were up on their feet.

'Paul! What in heaven's name has got into you?'

'The cross … give me the cross.'

'What?'

He hadn't the strength to argue. With arms wracked in pain he grabbed the priest's throat, feeling for the cross around his neck. 'Don't take Communion … poisoned.'

Father Willoughby struggled against the assault. 'Paul, have you lost your senses, that old story was something from half a century ago.'

'History repeats …'

'This is madness!'

Paul was starting to black out. 'Not your fault … this damn thing, evil …' The cross came away in his hands, and the pain that wracked his body made him want to scream.

Father Willoughby grabbed his arms, his face deathly white. 'God be with us!' he uttered.

A shudder reverberated through Paul's body. Pain vanished, the dark confusion lifted. Strength returned. Whatever had possessed him a moment ago, left him. 'I'm sorry for being so rough, Father.'

A blank look came into the priest's eyes, behind his glasses. Then, pushing past him, Father Willoughby ran down the aisle, vestments flapping, as if the devil itself was on his tail. Most of the congregation ran after him.

Paul turned, and dashed through to the vestry, searching through cupboards. It came as no real surprise to find a container of rat poison. He strode back through the now deserted church. The congregation had gathered outside and were staring upwards to the clock tower. Paul looked up too, and his heart sank.

The priest was clambering onto the battlement wall. Before Paul could make a move, he'd stretched his arms up to the sky and then slowly toppled forwards.

People screamed.

As the priest fell, Paul saw something streak upwards from his body. Something unbelievable; like a heat haze, shimmering, not transparent, but not solid, something unearthly in the vague shape of a winged figure – but not angelic, more demonic.

At that moment, a large bird flew directly through the shimmering haze seemingly sucking it up. One moment later, the vapour disappeared.

In the split second before Father Willoughby plunged to his death, Paul saw the expression on the priest's face change, the blankness replaced with a look of sheer terror. Then arms and legs circling wildly, he screamed briefly for God to help him. But it was too late.

The bird flew on into the forest, its crowing sounding now like laughter.

As people gathered around the priest, Paul walked slowly away. There was no point in waiting around for the police or the medics, no point at all. They couldn't stop this evil.

# Chapter 25

Back at the cottage, Paul gathered together every piece of wood that had come off that tree, the early efforts of fruit bowls and ornaments, the reclining nude, dust from the barn floor ... every last scrap of bark. He piled it all onto the bonfire, poured petrol from a can and lit a match.

'Mind your eyebrows!'

Paul spun round to see Owen striding down the garden with a bag full of what he guessed were his unsold carvings from the shop.

'What's all this about, then?' Owen asked, handing over the bag. 'Bit drastic, isn't it, burning all your stuff.'

Paul tipped the lot onto the fire. 'Owen, since you've been with Juliet, have you found yourself actually believing in witchcraft?'

'Not really, but I know it's something she likes to dabble with. Why?'

Paul explained – about Petronella, all the recent deaths, the splinter explosion at the Peace Conference and how he'd been manipulated by some sort of demonic presence that could possess people and make them do insane things such as Father Willoughby trying to poison his parishioners before leaping to his death.

Owen stood, open mouthed as sparks spat and wood flared from the bonfire. 'And you think Petronella was in the carvings?'

'I know she was. It's why the doctor's wife fell down the stairs, and the couple in their car. But it goes a long way further back, Owen. She had a hand in Helena's death too. I know it.'

Bluebell strolled up to Paul's ankles as he talked. The idea of the cat being anywhere near a bonfire bugged him. He picked it up.

'Let me just take her indoors.' He returned to see Owen sitting on the stump of a tree, staring into the flames.

'And you know, Owen,' continued Paul, 'I think this all stems from when we were kids, and I burned the witch's cat. She's never forgiven me.'

'Ah,' said Owen, looking sheepishly up. 'In which case, I've got something to confess.'

'That sounds ominous.'

'About that cat … the witch's cat.'

'Go on.'

'It wasn't you. It was me.'

Paul felt a sweep of darkness wash over him for a second. 'Owen, come with me.'

Owen followed him into the barn.

'See all these tools? I want you to put them into that box. I'm going to burn the lot. I'll get the axe.'

'Really? Owen frowned at him. 'You don't seem too upset about what I've just told you.'

'Just do what I've told you, and we'll discuss that later.'

'Okay, mate.'

Paul strode to the back of the barn and took the axe from the wall. Turning, he noticed Owen with his back to him, doing as he was asked. Paul took two silent steps towards him. He gripped the axe with both hands, swung it high above his shoulder and brought it swiftly down into the side of Owen's right kneecap.

A scream of agony filled the night. Owen collapsed onto his side, holding onto his bloodied leg, staring up in total shock. 'Paul … what the fuck …'

Without a word, Paul raised the axe again and brought it down onto his left leg, almost severing it but for a few ligaments hanging on.

Owen rolled onto his stomach, begging for mercy. 'Don't, don't hit me again. Please don't …'

Paul grabbed him by the back of his collar and dragged him outside, leaving behind a trail of blood. 'It was you!' he snarled. 'You, all this time. I thought it was *him!*'

'Who? Paul, mate. Help me, don't let me die.'

Dragging him over to the bonfire, Paul lifted Owen clean off the ground with one hand. Bringing him face to face so their noses almost touched, Paul uttered, 'You burned Theron, my cat. Now I burn you!'

With one thrust hurled Owen onto the bonfire.

The screams didn't last long.

Through Paul's eyes Lamia watched as the bonfire gradually died, leaving just the charred, distorted and twisted remains of Owen. Darkness descended over the garden, its silence only broken when a taxi pulled up outside the cottage. A car door shut and the lights from the patio shone out.

'Paul. Paul, I'm home. Is Owen with you?'

*Time to make her scream … again.*

'Yes, he's here. I'm coming.'

She smiled as he walked through the door. And then her smile vanished.

*How I love to play with humans. They are so soft and easy to break.*

Paul could hear Sally screaming. The sound came from far off, as if he were in a dream that he couldn't wake from. It was insane, and he could feel the sensations of having sex. His body was being used, he could feel Sally, and yet he couldn't. As if he was on another level, out of reach, unable to control his movements. As if someone or something had taken control of his mind and body.

There was a name echoing through his head; *Lamia. Lamia. Lamia.*

And Sally was screaming, and sobbing, and begging him to stop. And there was nothing he could do to stop it.

And then it was over.

Like in the hospital after the conference, confusion lifted, clarity returned leaving only a dull pain deep inside his skull – and shock at what lay before his eyes.

Sally hung over the sink, her clothing ripped to shreds. Wheals and bloodied scratch marks all down her back, blood trickling down her thighs.

'Sal …'

Slowly, she turned and faced him. Her face streaked in tears, bite marks on her breasts. 'Go,' she said.

'Sally … it was her.'

'Go!' she screamed at the top of her voice. 'Go!'

The witch was within him. Petronella, Lamia, whatever the name, it was certainly a witch. And there was only one way of killing a witch … He stopped his train of thought. He needed to work on automatic pilot, not thinking – doing. She was within him, he had no doubt, he needed to control his thoughts, not give away any inkling of what he needed to do.

Putting distance between him and Sally was paramount, He snatched her car keys and ran out of the cottage, her sobs breaking his heart.

Outside, something caught his eye. The glowing embers of a bonfire. He could smell something, smells reminiscent of a barbecue on a summer's day. He hadn't been out here cooking. He'd been out here burning his carvings, and Owen had turned up …

His old friend's car was still parked by the wall.

Bile was rising in his throat as he walked towards the hot ashes. When he saw the blackened carcass he wretched violently. Tears streamed down his face.

'Bastard!' he screamed into the night.

Autopilot clicked in. Years of training, mind over matter clicked into place. Torture training, he'd always thought of it. Blanking out everything of importance. Concentrating on the mundane. Give nothing away.

He picked up the things he needed, turned and walked back to the car.

Automatically, he headed towards London. Radio on, loud. He sang along, at the top of his voice. Mile upon mile flew by.

At some point in his journey, his mobile rang, vibrating in his pocket. He took it out, glanced at the screen – Daniel Rake.

He would answer. Natural for him to answer. 'Paul Christian.'

'Paul!'

'Speaking.'

'Paul, for God's sake, man … tell me where you are.'

'Driving.'

'Sally rang me. Paul, tell me where you are. I'll come and get you. You're sick. We'll get you some treatment …'

He hung up, throwing the mobile onto the passenger seat. He ignored the next two calls. No more followed.

He directed his thoughts back to training. Sergeant Johnston had been a sadistic bastard to cadets. 'Move it, Christian. Move it!' He could feel his spittle on his face. He could feel the weight of his backpack bouncing on his spine.

Paul drove, music blaring – Sergeant Johnston bellowing in his head.

Headlights in his mirror meant nothing. London's roads were chaotic. He noted the shape, knew what make of car it was following him. Guessed who the driver was.

'Keep it moving, Christian, you weak little runt.'

He pressed his foot down on the accelerator, weaving between the cars. Headlights followed, then were lost amongst the chaos of London's streets.

He drew the car to a halt by the river. Got out, took the can. 'Stop snivelling Christian. Concentrate on me, Christian! You pathetic excuse for a soldier.' Spittle splashed into his face.

An expanse of grey river ran in front of him, stone wall, stone steps, black leather shoes running down each step. No! Army boots, size twelve, and Johnston's voice bellowing, 'Call them press ups, Christian? My mother could do better …'

He untwisted the lid from the can. The smell of petrol filled his nose and a sudden pain shot through his temples. He reached into his memories and brought Sergeant Johnston back to the forefront of his thoughts. 'Move it, Christian!'

'Move it, Christian,' he repeated out loud, lifting the can, spilling the liquid over his head, soaking himself in petrol.

He heard it shriek from inside him. Felt it writhe, clawing at his arm from the inside to stop him.

Someone else was shouting his name. Rake. He glimpsed Daniel Rake and Fitzpatrick peering over the wall.

Within him, Paul felt its power explode inside, clawing at his hand from inside of him, a battle of wills as blackness swamped his consciousness. He struck the match.

'Paul, no!' Rake's voice rang out.

As a wall of flame shot up, Paul glimpsed Rake and Fitzpatrick running hell for leather towards him.

It shrieked inside of him. He sensed its swirling terror as flame engulfed them both. 'Die, bitch,' he uttered, as heat scorched his throat.

Something else appeared through the flames – his darling Helena, smiling at him, arms reaching out to take him away from this ball of flame.

Then something slammed against him, knocking him off his feet. The dark waters of the Thames rushed up to meet him, and with the shock of the cold, so another shock-wave flashed through him – an entity vacating his body, shooting out of him.

He saw it, before water flooded over his head, and as the hiss of steam rose all around him, he saw it – the shimmering haze of evil, hovering against the grey of night – winged and demonic, powerful and hateful.

Someone was shouting. Fitzpatrick's voice, 'What the hell is that?'

Before Paul sank below the surface, he heard another sound, that of wings beating. A raven, black as night, swooped down, flying straight through the demonic spirit, sucking it up into its sleek body. It flew on, into the darkness of the night.

No! Paul silently screamed, as the blackness of icy water swamped him, and oblivion claimed him.

# Chapter 26

Flickering lights and hospital smells confirmed to Paul that he was still alive. Slowly as his surroundings came into focus, he thought he was nine years old again. He was all wired up, his throat felt parched, and it felt like gauze dressing covered most of his body.

He looked around for the deflated birthday balloons. There were none. He glanced to his side, expecting his parents to be there. They weren't, but Fitzpatrick was.

He jumped up and pressed a buzzer. Moments later a doctor and nurse came in, followed by Daniel Rake.

They told him the medically induced coma was to alleviate the pain and give his body time to heal. Paul didn't need to ask them any other questions, he remembered everything.

There was no point telling them they should have let him die, taking the demon – witch, whatever it was, with him. It had referred to itself as Lamia. He wondered how many others Lamia had possessed over the ages. Petronella had been a victim just like him. Just a poor sod that Lamia took over to control and spread her evil.

There would be no convincing anyone, though. No one would believe such evil existed.

By now they would have discovered Owen's body. Tears swam in his eyes for his old pal. And Sally … poor Sally.

His heart ached.

He wouldn't get prison. Diminished responsibility. They'd just lock him up in a secure hospital and pump him full of drugs.

'Can you hear me, Paul?' Daniel Rake said softly.

'Yes,' he uttered.

'We saw it.'

Paul stared through the slits in the gauze covering his face.

Daniel Rake moved closer to him, Fitzpatrick too.

'We both saw it.'

Paul blinked. 'What did you see?'

'The witch,' Rake whispered. 'It was like a heat haze but in the shape of a winged angel.'

'No angel,' Paul said, struggling to get the words out. 'Devil.'

'And,' added Fitzpatrick, 'some of the parishioners at the church where the priest jumped, reported seeing a similar vision.'

He stared at them, a flicker of hope rising within him. 'So, I'm not insane,' Paul croaked.

'No, and you're not to blame for Owen's death. You were possessed by some demonic force,' said Rake. 'I gather that's why you set fire to yourself.'

'It was the only way. Only now it's free again. It would have been better if you'd let me burn. It was the only way to destroy it.'

'As if I'd stand there and let you burn yourself alive,' said Rake, his eyes narrowed at the thought of it. Then he smiled. 'The Thames was bloody cold though.'

Paul nodded.

Rake looked steadily at Paul. 'We need to tell you something. The splinters from the bust – they seemed superficial, at first. But since then every one of those politicians has been behaving crazily. They're making bad decisions, as if they're deliberately antagonising other countries. Believe me, world peace seems to be taking a downward spiral.'

Paul rested his head back on his pillow, understanding now. Lamia's hatred wasn't just for him, it was for everyone, the whole of mankind.

'She's working for the devil,' he managed to croak. 'She wants to destroy everyone. And I think I know her name.'

Rake stared at him. 'You do?'

'I think it's Lamia.'

'I believe you, Paul,' Rake said softly. 'But we're not going to sit by and let it happen. There's a special team at HQ being set up to look into the phenomena. We need you well, Paul. We need you to tell us all you know. We'll destroy it, but we need your help.'

They both stared at him, waiting for his answer.

Though it hurt to move, he nodded.

'Good man.'

'Yes, he is a good man.'

Sally's voice. Sally's sweet voice right here in his room. His eyes flicked from right to left, trying to see beyond Rake and Fitzpatrick who were huddled around him.

They moved aside and he saw his lovely Sally walk into his line of vision.

He uttered a cry, wanting to reach out and hold her, and tell her how sorry he was.

She sat beside him on the bed.

Through eyes blurred with tears, he managed to rasp out some speech.

'Sal, so sorry.'

'You have nothing to be sorry for, Paul. It wasn't you. I knew it wasn't you.'

Very gently, she took his bandaged hand in hers, and brought it to her lips.

## The End

*uge thanks to the great team at Bloodhound Books.*
***Robert & Ann***

Lightning Source UK Ltd.
Milton Keynes UK
UKHW04f0625150718
325723UK00001B/68/P